Sequoia Shootout

Sequoia Shootout

JOHN REESE

DOUBLEDAY & COMPANY, INC.

GARDEN CITY, NEW YORK

1977

All of the characters in this book
are fictitious, and any resemblance
to actual persons, living or dead,
is purely coincidental.

First Edition

ISBN: 0-385-12693-X
Library of Congress Catalog Card Number 76–29792
Copyright © 1977 by John Reese
All Rights Reserved
Printed in the United States of America

For my old buddy Buck Johnson

Sequoia Shootout

CHAPTER I

The shriek of a bullet, and his ratty old black hat went flying. Instinct and habit—no one who had ever heard that sound would do anything else—made him tumble from his horse in a head-first dive. As he hit the ground he could only hope to God that the horse would not run off and take the pack horses with it.

They ran, but not too far. He lay there a moment, controlling his breath, trying by sheer force of will to slow the beat of his pounding heart. It was not easy. Defeat, frustration and the worst discouragement of his life had him close to the end of his physical and mental reserves. He felt dirty, beaten, lean as a whip snake and mean as a tarantula.

Nothing happened.

He squirmed an inch at a time to where he could see over the edge of the shallow gully into which he had—luckily—been unhorsed. The first thing he saw was his worthless old hat. The slug had caught its worn and wilted peak, shredding it but missing his skull by a good three inches. Well, he thought, there goes sixty cents shot to hell. . . .

The second thing he saw was a man riding off to the west as hard as a big, rawboned brown horse could take him. Under the rider's arm a rifle was balanced, a big one. He had the range, the power, and the weight of the slug, and yet he was fogging out of there, fast. Did he think he had killed his man with that one shot?

Jefferson Hewitt stood up slowly, shaking his head. No, the son of a bitch was looking back over his shoulder as though he knew he had missed. Looking straight into the rising sun, which was just lifting above the horizon now.

Good shooting, with the sun in his eyes. Then why quit cold?

Gaunt, unshaven, exhausted as much by the feeling of defeat as by months of endless exertion, Hewitt picked up his worthless old hat and caught his horse. On his saddle hung a Remington .30-30 in a boot. It was one of his favorite guns, but the fleeing sniper had him outgunned. And this desert's rocky hills and gullies had a lot of hiding places in them. The next shot would not be against a glaring, early-dawn sun.

Hewitt trembled all over as he climbed into the saddle. Part of that was sheer hunger, but he could do nothing about it and he had long ago learned not to fret away his strength on things he could not help. The thing to do was make sure nobody got a second shot at him.

The pack horses followed as he turned southward, carrying the .30-30 under his left arm. The first rays of the sun felt nice, nice. It was April, but the nights were still cold at this elevation on the Nevada mesa. The sun helped him stop trembling, too.

Shortly he turned west again, riding slowly, stopping often to search the terrain ahead of him. He had, however, a deep and firm conviction that no one was lurking there for a second shot. All Durango Slim had wanted, once he touched off that one shot, was to put a lot of trail behind him.

He had never met Durango Slim—had never even seen him until just now—and yet he could not have known a brother better. The bastard was a deadly shot and a killer, but he was yellow all the way through. A coward can be dangerous even in a stand-up, face-to-face fight, on a hot day, with an audience, and above all with the secret confidence that he was the better shot.

But it took a different kind of nerve to lie in wait and shoot it out in the cold morning, after a long, cold night. Having the range, muzzle velocity and superior weight of bullet then was not enough to make up for the hollowness of cowardice.

Jefferson Hewitt came to the spot from which the sniper had fired. He did not have to dismount to read the sign. Durango Slim must have squatted there most of the night, less than half a mile from where Hewitt had spent the night. He had smoked one cigarette after another. His horse had been tied to that ocotillo yonder. Not until daylight showed him Hewitt coming toward him, not until a showdown was forced on him, had he dared to fire.

Good old Durango Slim!

Hewitt almost smiled—almost, but not quite. His own night had been spent in a dry, cold camp where there was thick winter grass for his horses. He might have dozed a moment now and then, leaning against a rock that still held a little heat from yesterday, the Remington across his lap. Had the son of a bitch only come on foot, a few hundred yards farther on the back trail—

That was the kind of guts Durango Slim lacked. He could beat a fifteen-year-old girl to death with his fists, but he could not face another grown man even when he had the bigger gun.

Again Hewitt left the trail. He wasted miles because of that bigger gun, because he did not trust even Durango Slim's cowardice. It was against his whole nature, as Hewitt

knew that nature, but he *could* have nerved himself to wait
for one more shot.

He had not. The sun mounted above the horizon and lay
there a moment, a burning ball on a slack string. Hewitt
had it over his right shoulder when he first saw the dying
gold camp of Kelly's Ravine. It was a mile to the north of
him, sprawled along the narrow gully that gave it a name,
on a southern slope.

Men were already stirring on their claims. There was
only one wooden building, though it was a big one, and
there were only three horses in sight. They were tied behind
the wooden building, haltered to a low-box wagon full of
hay. Hewitt pulled up and studied the camp for a long time.

Then he rode on, confident that Durango Slim was no
threat this morning. The girl-killer had no place to hide this
side of the gold camp, and he would never risk a second
shot around witnesses. Hewitt's horse wanted to run. He let
it run, the pack horses breaking into a trot beneath their
light packs behind him.

For a moment, Hewitt hoped again. For a few heart-
beats he had his guts back and could believe that his luck
could not always be all bad. But he was too thin and ragged
and tired and hungry to be himself for long.

He dismounted and led his saddle horse up the gully
through the camp, the pack horses following faithfully. He
did not speak, feeling the rage build up in him, but men
got out of his way and did not welcome him. No man in-
vited a "Hidy" who had the look in his eye that Hewitt had.
Here comes a bad one. Why bother him?

Jeff Hewitt was a man of average height, dressed now
like a saddle tramp. A month's growth of brownish beard
obscured the stiff brown mustache he always wore. Under
his shabby jacket he wore a Colt .45 in a holster of his own

design. The gun lay almost horizontally, an easy grab, held by a pawl that gripped the front sight. A slight twist, part of the natural movement of drawing it, freed the gun in shooting position.

Hewitt was never out of practice. He was not as good a shot as he was reputed to be—no man was that good—but he was pretty good. In a shoulder holster he wore a .38. In his hip pocket, the right-hand one where he carried his handkerchief, he carried a shot-filled leather sap. He was a devout believer in the sap as a much-neglected weapon and he was pretty good with it, too.

Hewitt was eighteen or twenty pounds underweight, down to gristle, bone and nerve. And as he lost heart again, as he raged silently through Kelly's Ravine, leading his horse, he was telling himself, Well, I'm whipped. He got away again. For the first time in my life, by God, I come up loser. . . .

He had lost everything except his guns and his sap last month, fording the Colorado River. His horse, his pack mule and a stray dog that had attached itself to him in Utah had drowned. The two Chemehuevi Indians who had warned him not to try it had fished him out. He should have listened to them. It was their country, their river. He had been out of his mind to try it.

But he had been *so* sure he was near the end of a long, ugly trail! He had never heard Durango Slim's real name and, along about then, he had even stopped thinking of him as Durango Slim. The girl-killer. That was what had warped his mind and judgment, the idea of being so close to the murderer of a girl of fifteen.

It had cost him a mint to buy the three new horses, the saddle and pack saddles and tarps, the blankets, the skillet and coffee pot, the Remington. It had cost him a week, too, and a chance to catch up with the girl-killer. Wherefore he raged silently through Kelly's Ravine to get it out of his system, and found himself still full of it.

He knew to a cent how much money he had in his pocket: nine ten-dollar gold eagles, three double eagles, a five-dollar bill, two ones and $1.80 in small change. Total, $158.80, and he still had to eat, get warm, and then get over the Sierra Nevada—fast.

A guide who knew the Sierra passes would come high. Everything came high in a mining camp, especially when it started to die. A month ago there had been, he had heard, five thousand men in Kelly's Ravine. Now there were fewer than a thousand. The winter rains were over. The stream fed by the desert spring, which alone made placer mining possible, had dwindled to a trickle. Soon it would dry up entirely, for the summer.

Give this camp another month and the last embittered gold-seeker would be gone. And next winter, silky sleeper grass would cover the scars gophered out by the miners' shovels—if, that is, it rained. The desert was full of such dead camps. They were the burial places of dead hopes, of hopes that had never really been born.

He stopped at the big wooden building. It was windowless, built of redwood slabs and battens with a tar-paper roof. Over the narrow door was a sign neatly painted in black on red:

SAM BERRY'S SALOON
Drinks, Eats and Games

Sam Berry. He wished he could remember where he had heard that name. Men were pouring out of Sam Berry's place, shivering in the morning chill. They had been drinking and playing poker all night, and if there was a winner

among them, his face did not betray him. Now they had to
go back to another brutal, losing game, trying to wash gold
out of the gravel of Kelly's Ravine.

Hewitt was so hungry he was suddenly swallowing his
own spit. He had to eat at whatever cost. Losing dulled a
man's judgment. So did anger. So did haste, so did anxiety
—and so did hunger.

He tied his saddle horse to the corner of the building and
tied the pack horses to his saddle horn. As he turned toward the door, he felt someone take his arm.

"Sure an' it's Mr. Laidlaw," said a hoarse voice with a
thick Irish brogue. "'Tis a long time, sir. But ye do
remember me, don't ye, Mr. Laidlaw?"

A big, beer-bellied man with a sunburned face marbled
by alcohol was looking at him with desperation in his eyes.
He looked sixty and was probably forty-five. It was eleven
years since Hewitt had seen him, and how he had decayed!

"Why," he said, "it's Sergeant Peter O'Hara of Troop L,
isn't it? Of course I remember you."

"I've been out of the service eight years now," the man
said, humbly, "and I lost me stripes before I'd time to get
used to 'em, sir."

"Too bad."

"'Tis life. Ye look like ye'd fell on hard times yerself,
Mr. Laidlaw."

"Well, you know the horse business," Hewitt said. "Make
a dollar today, lose two tomorrow. And the name, by the
way, is Hewitt, Jefferson Hewitt."

The big Irishman scowled at him blankly, trying to understand. "But sir, 'twas yerself found the evidince to clear
Major Foos intirely at his court-martial, God rest his soul.
He's dead now, ye know. But if I can remimber that, how
could I fergit your own name, sir?"

Peter O'Hara was suffering with the awful hangover of a prolonged spree. He was a pest, but he was lonely for human contact, for one decent word from another person. Hewitt could not make himself get rid of him.

"It's a long story, Peter, and it'll have to wait until another day. I'm sorry about Major Foos. He was a good man."

"The best sir. He fought us hard, but he tuk good care of us, too. What're ye doin' here, sir?"

"Not stopping. On my way to Sacramento."

"Only Carson Pass would be open yet, ye know. It's been an early melt, but the others—Tioga and Donner especially —won't be open until June."

"I've got to find someone who can guide me, Peter. Where'll I find someone?"

O'Hara tried to stand at attention. "No one knows the passes like meself, sir. I ran me own string of pack mules through the Sierra for five years afther leavin' the Army. I can get ye through."

Hewitt had another of those irrational changes of mood. From bottomless despair he soared breathlessly to shining hope. O'Hara might be a drunk, but he had never been a brag or a liar.

"By God, if you can do that, then my luck has turned!" he almost shouted. "When could we leave?"

"Anny time ye say, sir."

"Today?"

"I've nathin' holdin' me here by the seat o' me britches."

I'm gaining on him, Hewitt thought. Now I'm on a hot trail again. My luck has come back, and it's this big, drunken ex-trooper that will put the girl-killer in my hands. Soon!

CHAPTER II

"Come have breakfast with me, Peter," Hewitt said, "and make some plans. My treat."

O'Hara held back as Hewitt tugged at his arm. "Sorry, sir, but I'm not welcome to Sam Berry's place."

"Why not?"

"A bit of a fight, sir. Two or three, really."

"Nonsense! You're my guest, and my money is as good as anybody's."

"I—I can't, sir. I'd only get the hired help in trouble wid Sam. I know me place, sir."

Hewitt took him by the upper arm and shoved him violently through the door. "Any friend of mine has the right to walk through any door, Peter. Nobody turns down my guest or my money—nobody!"

Inside, the lanterns still fought the thick tobacco smoke that had been accumulating all night. Sam Berry's place would have made a fair sheep shed—just a fair one— anywhere else. To their left as they entered was a plank bar tended by one exhausted man. To their right were eight poker tables, all empty now.

Across the rear of the building ran a plank serving counter, behind which was a crude kitchen. A weary, half-crippled cook, no doubt hired from some ranch cook-wagon after last fall's roundup, yawned as he mopped his hotplate down with a greasy rag.

"What can you give us for breakfast?" Hewitt asked him.

The cook turned, his face becoming surly. "Ham and fried spuds is all I got," he said, "but I can't serve O'Hara, and he damn well knows it."

"Come on, man, he's my guest. I'm responsible for him. What's the price of breakfast?"

"Dollar and a half, but like I told you, O'Hara ain't allowed in here. If you want to make trouble, you can get the hell out yourself."

Hewitt felt, joyfully, a twitch of temper. It was unfair to blame the old flunky for following orders, but when you had a job to do you started at the starting place. Hewitt put his five-dollar bill on the counter.

"Three dollars for two breakfasts," he said softly, "a dollar for yourself, and you owe me one."

"No!"

"Tell the boss I made you serve us at gunpoint. I can do that, my friend, if I have to."

The cook looked past him. Hewitt spun on his heel and saw a big, beefy man with shoulders like the end of a railroad boxcar striding toward them. He carried some middle-aged fat, but Hewitt would have bet he could be his own bouncer in the toughest saloon in the world. If Peter O'Hara had problems for him, it was a tribute to Peter.

"Tell them, Mr. Berry," the cook said. "Tell them I ain't supposed to feed this goddamn O'Hara."

Berry gave Hewitt a civil nod. "That's right, he isn't, stranger," he said. "O'Hara knows he's not welcome here. Glad to feed you if you've got the money to pay for it, but I'll not let this bum break my place up again."

"Did you break up the place, Peter?" Hewitt asked, and when O'Hara nodded, Hewitt looked back, scornfully, at Berry. "How much damage did he do? How much could he do? You haven't got twenty dollars' worth of furniture here."

"That ain't the point. If people get the idea they can come in here and—"

Hewitt interrupted: "Oh, cut it out. That's part of the business of running a gold-camp saloon, and if you're not man enough to police the place, close it up. I'll be responsible for O'Hara today. Is my money good, or not?"

Berry's big face reddened. "Not now. Out, both of you —out quietly—out, out!"

He reached to take Hewitt's wrist in the bouncer's come-along grip. Once the bouncer got it, you came along or you got your wrist broken. Hewitt side-stepped quickly and said, "Stay out of this, Peter."

If Sam Berry had not been working all night, if he had been wide awake and had not lost his temper, he would have been too much man for Hewitt. He made another grab, and his enormous hand moved like a sidewinder's head. He turned as he grabbed, to tuck Hewitt's hand under his own wrist.

Hewitt's hand darted out with the shot-filled sap in it. He snapped it rather than swung it, and he caught Berry sharply on the elbow.

"Ai-i-i-i-i," Berry moaned. He clutched at the elbow with his left hand and bent over, gritting his teeth against the pain.

Hewitt slid the sap back into his pocket and took the .45 from under his coat. "This," he said, "has gone far enough. Do you want me to fire a couple through your roof, Mr. Berry? How many friends do you think you have here? These people are sore as hell. If there's any gold in Kelly's Ravine, you've got it. How long do you think it would take me to organize a lynching party?"

Berry leaned against the nearest poker table and tried flexing the fingers of his right hand. "You busted my elbow," he said, through his teeth.

"Nonsense. It'll be tender for a day or two, but I could have killed you, partner. I came in here to spend money with my friend. I think you've lost this pot. Why should we have any more trouble?"

Berry was already able to shake his numb hand without agony. Feeling seemed to come back to it one finger at a time. He ignored Hewitt to look at the cook.

"Go ahead, feed them," he said. "Fella's right—who wants trouble this early in the day?"

He went behind the serving counter and out the back door, shaking the feeling back into his hand. The cook prodded his fire and put in some more piñon knots, heavy with thick, combustible pitch.

"Plenty of coffee to start," Hewitt said.

"Help yourself," the cook replied. "Come back for your grub in a couple of minutes."

Hewitt carried the heavy coffee mugs to one of the poker tables, but O'Hara was in bad shape. He fell to one knee when he tried to sit down. Hewitt had to help him to his feet, and then O'Hara could not trust his shaking hands to pick up the hot coffee.

Hewitt held it for him and let him take two sips. "No, Peter, more," he said, when the Irishman shook his head. "Get this stuff down you. We're going to talk business."

He had to cut O'Hara's ham for him when the waiter brought the two platters heaped high with food. O'Hara could not manage a fork, but he picked up his spoon and got a bite or two down.

Hewitt held the coffee for him again, and made him take most of it. "Eat!" he commanded.

"Sir, why are ye botherin' wid the likes of me?"

The poor devil needed more than food. "Because you're my luck," Hewitt said.

"How's that, sir?"

"My luck changed the very second I met you, Peter. I've been on a three months' losing streak. When you told me you could get me through the Sierra Nevada passes, it was like filling a flush. You used to be a hell of a man, you know."

"Not now, sir. Not no more."

"Maybe. But maybe you're a lucky one from now on, and sometimes that's better. Eat!"

The hangdog gratitude in O'Hara's eyes was worth all the trouble. Hewitt sat down and began to eat. Suddenly O'Hara began feeding ravenously, scooping it in with the spoon as though he had not had a square meal in months. And that, Hewitt thought, was probably the case.

The cook appeared at their table. "Everything all right?"

"Just fine, thanks," Hewitt said. "You're a good cook."

"Not much you can do with ham and spuds."

"You can ruin them. Some cooks do. I have never tasted better than this."

Everybody needed appreciation, respect. The cook looked almost as grateful as O'Hara, but then he seemed to remember what he had come to do.

"Ever been in Omaha?"

"Many times," said Hewitt. "Why?"

"For instance, when that man burned down the Star Hotel and the clothing store that went with it?"

"I believe I recall that, yes."

"Damn right you do. You were the goddamn Pinkerton that put the burner in jail."

"Friend of yours, was he?"

"No, but I don't like Pinkertons. You drove a fine rented buggy and dressed like a sport, but you was a goddamn Pinkerton and I didn't like you then and I don't like you now."

"A couple of points to set the record straight. One: I'm not a Pinkerton. And two: There were three men that burned to death in that fire. Just bums sleeping in the coal room, but they could have been the three of us. I don't see what you're trying to prove."

The cook dropped two silver dollars on the table. "This. I don't take tips from Pinkertons."

Hewitt stood up and kicked his chair back. "I told you that I'm not a Pinkerton, and I'm getting tired of this. I don't like to mistreat a good old man, but if you don't pick one of those dollars up and put it in your pocket, you and I are going to lock horns."

The cook seemed satisfied. Perhaps he was even a little pleased at being threatened with a fight, after all these years. "Well, hell, if it means that much to you," he said.

He pocketed one of the dollars and returned to his kitchen. O'Hara finished eating and leaned closer.

"He'll tell Sam you're a Pinkerton," he whispered. "Sam may come in wid a gun, sir. It's sorry I am that I got ye into trouble."

"Nobody gets me into trouble, Peter—nobody but me," said Hewitt. "And I get myself out of it, too."

He ate more slowly. If O'Hara thought Sam Berry would be back, it was pretty certain that Sam Berry would be back. And in a couple of minutes, he was.

"Mind if I sit a minute?" he asked.

"You're very welcome, Mr. Berry," said Hewitt.

Berry sat down. "My cook claims that you're a Pinkerton."

"I'm not."

The saloonkeeper rubbed his sore elbow, but he seemed to carry no grudge. "Suit yourself, but if you're looking for anybody special, a deputy United States marshal spent the night here. He pulled out early this morning, well before daylight."

"Looking for anybody in particular?"

"Don't know. Just thought I'd tell you."

Hewitt nodded. "I can't imagine being interested in anyone sought by a federal officer right now, but thanks very much. I'm on my way to Sacramento and Peter tells me he can get me through. Can he?"

"If anybody can, he can." He grinned suddenly, showing a mouthful of gold teeth. "It will be a relief to get Peter out of camp. Maybe it will help get him off the crock for a while. He's a good man when he's sober. I'll be glad to serve you any way I can."

"One thing," said Hewitt. "I wonder if a man by the name of Durango Slim has been through here?"

"Why, hell, he's been running my poker tables for almost a month," Berry exclaimed. "Left early last evening to take a ride and never showed up. Now they tell me his horse is gone, too. Reckon the marshal was after him?"

"I have no idea."

"Funny thing is," Berry said, frowning, "if he don't come back, he's out some money. I was paying him thirty dollars a night. Can you imagine that? Thirty dollars, and I owe him four nights' pay. Why would he walk on a hundred and twenty dollars?"

Hewitt said, carefully, "I wouldn't want to guess, but if he does return, I believe I'd have the money ready to pay him."

"That I will. Ever see him shoot that rifle of his? It's a

Winchester Model Seventy-three, and he can drive nails with it as far as he can see them."

Hewitt said nothing. They studied each other in silence a moment before Berry blurted, "I wonder what he's wanted for. He's a mean son of a bitch, I'll tell you that. I don't think he said a pleasant word to anybody in camp except over the cards."

Suddenly Hewitt remembered where he had heard this man's name. "Used to be a Sam Berry who ran a store and trading point in Indian Territory," he said, "not far from the Kansas line. Would that be you, sir?"

"It would."

"Got run out of town, I heard." Berry said nothing, but his expression froze and his eyes narrowed and glinted. Hewitt went on, "Story I got, there was a sporting house across the tracks from you. I forget the name of the place, but she got some girls in that you thought were too young to—"

Berry interrupted with, "I cleaned the place out, if that's what you mean, and that same night I got burned out. Pinkerton man, I've run saloons from Kansas City to Cripple Creek to Yuma, and I ain't no missionary. But there's some things I won't stand for and I don't apologize to nobody."

Hewitt nodded and leaned back in his chair. "Know what a recruiter is in the white slave trade, Mr. Berry?"

"Hell yes, of course, but I don't see—"

"Reason I want to talk to Durango Slim," Hewitt said, "is that he may be in the same business."

It was Berry's turn to lean back in his chair. The two men looked at each other silently a moment. Then Berry said, "He kept his nose clean here. You'll notice there's no sporting house in Kelly's Ravine, and never was. How sure are you of your facts?"

"Far from sure. I don't even know the man. You do. Do you think it's a possibility?"

"I reckon. But what was he doing here?"

"If I'm right about him, he needed a stake. It takes money to seduce young girls, run off with them and make hookers of them. Lots of profit in it, too, but like any profitable business, it takes capital."

"Well, Durango Slim's got it now. I paid him thirty dollars a night. He won some big games on his own time. He should have a couple of thousand dollars, and he's got a good horse and some good clothes. If I'd had any idee the son of a bitch was in that trade—"

Berry choked on his own anger. Hewitt said, "I need another saddle and bridle. Either of my pack horses will make Peter a good saddle horse."

"I've got bridles, and I've got a good McClellan saddle and I don't reckon Peter would ride any other. Any other way I could help you?"

"We'll need a little grub."

"You'll get it." Berry stared into the corner a long time, at nothing. "I only wish I could be there when you catch up with Durango Slim," he said, at length. "I reckon maybe you'd be more than he'd want to try to handle, sir."

"Well, I might try to handle him."

Berry seemed to come awake. "I didn't. He stole me blind and I knew it and couldn't catch him at it. You expect them to knock down a little, but not like him, and I couldn't prove it on him!"

"And you didn't really want to."

"No, sir. To be honest, maybe it was yellow of me, but I didn't want a showdown with Durango Slim. Not many men I'm scared of, but I've been around the track a few times, and I know when to go to the whip and when to lose gracefully. And I just felt—somehow I *knew*—that here was a mean, cold, brutal son of a bitch that was too much for me. So if that was yellow—"

"Not yellow," said Hewitt, "just smart. Best hunch you ever bet in your life."

CHAPTER III

It would be good to get up into the trees, into the clean air of the higher elevations. It would be cold up there. They had some hard climbing ahead of them, and he wished he had time to sleep about twenty hours and eat a peck before tackling it. Since he could not, it would be healing, in its way, to be up in the big timber.

O'Hara rode in front, followed by the pack horses. Hewitt brought up the rear. O'Hara had vomited up his breakfast as he cinched up the pack horse in his careful and highly professional way. He looked ghastly when they set out, but Sam Berry had given him several pounds of dry, leathery jerky.

Now O'Hara sat straight in the saddle, like the old cavalryman he was, chewing away on jerky and leaning over now and then to study the clearly marked trail to the west. Kelly's Ravine was far behind them and the ascending slope was growing steeper.

O'Hara must have been a good pack train operator. The pack on the horse ahead of Hewitt had not shifted an inch, nor had the short-handled shovel that rode on top of it. He was probably a hopeless drunk, but he was a man of talents, and there was something about him that Hewitt liked. At the bottom he was a kind, decent man, and maybe this was what had made him vulnerable to the world and had driven him to escape into whiskey.

O'Hara stopped his horse, turned in the saddle, and motioned for Hewitt to ride forward. "Two horses ahead of us," he said. "Both shod all around, sir. I think I know Durango Slim's horse. He's behint the other man."

"The deputy United States marshal that Sam Berry told us about," Hewitt said.

"Surely."

O'Hara looked like the wrath of God. "Peter," Hewitt said, "do you need a shot to steady your nerves? I've got a full pint in the pack, you know."

"I saw it, sir, but I'm off it for life," O'Hara said, bleakly, in a hoarse, hangover voice. "Nary another drop to the end of me days, and this time I mean it, and I'll thank yez not to laugh at me when I say it, sir."

"I'm not laughing, but you know it'll be worse tomorrow."

"Yes, but someday it'll get better. I'm a man who cannot take one drink, sir, and now I know it. Up there is me peace of mind, sir. When I'm up in the high passes, somehow I don't miss the drink. Oh—now and then, maybe, but whin I'm up there I only touch me beads when the desire hits me, and I'm well again."

He pointed up to the blue-green mass of pines, visible above the scattered softwood trees around them, and took his rosary from his pocket. The look he gave Hewitt was ashamed but not stupid.

"I know how you feel," said Hewitt. "Some people feel that the ocean heals them."

"Not I, sir."

"Nor I. But I've got over many a misery up in the big timber."

"Then ye do understand. Have ye ever seen the big ones? I forget their name, but the really big trees."

"The sequoias?"

"Yis. Not the Coast redwoods, but the others."

"I've seen only the Coast variety."

"I'd like to get up to the South Grove again. 'Tis like a cathedral there, sir. Or maybe not. Maybe 'tis more what the men had in mind when they built the cathedrals, and couldn't quite make it come true."

There were two varieties that came under the name of "redwood": *Sequoia sempervirens,* which grew along the Pacific coast and was the most valuable timber tree in the world, and *Sequoia gigantea,* the biggest trees in the world, most of which which grew at around an altitude of 4,000 to 5,000 feet. When a Westerner said "big tree," he meant *gigantea,* and someday Hewitt meant to see them.

"Once we've dealt with Durango Slim," he said, "we'll take a couple of weeks off and go see your South Grove."

O'Hara nodded dreamily. "Huks," he muttered. "Cleve Huks. No mistake about it, sir, that's him."

"What?"

"That's Durango Slim's name, Cleve Huks."

Hewitt could only stare. "You know him?"

"Used to, since he was a bit of a boyo. He didn't know me, old soak that I am, but I knew him."

It was easy to take a drunk's talk too seriously, but Hewitt believed him. "I told you, Peter, you're my luck," he said. "How did you happen to know him? What do you know about him? Man, this could be life or death to me!"

"Why," O'Hara said, "when I first j'ined up, in the old Eighth, Jan Huks was the sergeant that made a sojer of me. A Hollander, sir, an' a dacent, sober man married to a good woman an' savin' of his money. When they had four kids and money enough, Jan tuk up homestead land in Red Willow County, Nebraska.

"Cleve was the youngest, although they had two more later. All good children but Cleve. He'd already went bad when me troop stopped at Jan's place to rest and water our mounts a few years afther. 'Twas hard for old Jan to talk about it, but he did to me."

"In what way had he gone bad, Peter?"

"The usual. Tuk to drunkenness, gamblin', an' afther the girls. He'd just run off with a neighbor girl, a Bohemian girl only fourteen."

Hewitt had to control the trembling that threatened to shake his whole body. "Know what happened to him after that?"

"Well, sir, I ran into him in the troubles wid the Arapahoes in Colorado soon after. He didn't know me, sir, but I knew him. He'd no girl wid him then, so if he's white slavin', likely that's what went wid her."

Hewitt questioned him closely. The man O'Hara knew as Cleve Huks would be about thirty now. Average height, but good shoulders, and thick legs and arms, and quick on his feet. The kind of adenoidy good looks that a certain kind of restless, witless girl or woman might find irresistible. Pale hair, icy blue eyes, flattish face with a flattish nose and full, almost girlish mouth.

"Peter," said Hewitt, "he's heading hell-bent for Sacramento. I don't want to arrive too far behind him, but neither do I want to get close enough for him to know I'm on his trail. I've followed him for months. He has seen me, but I've had only distant glimpses of him. He'll know me instantly—I may or may not know him."

O'Hara, with something to exercise his mind, had lost the blankly stupid expression of a hung-over drunk. "It may not be aisy to time it, sir. Cleve's brown gelding is a looker, but I don't think he's much horse—and Cleve don't know the passes. Know what I think?"

"No, what?"

"His worthless horse will play out on the climb. The deputy marshal is ridin' a good horse. He's ahead of Huks, but not so far that Huks can't catch up. He'll half kill his horse to go around him and lay in wait. Or if he only gets in range with that Winchester of his . . ."

"Is he that good with it?"

"The best I've ever seen, sir. That's a forty-four-caliber gun, sir, and I'd not want to be well mounted on the trail ahead of him when Huks's horse begins to play out. I'm not too far gone in the whiskey to be useful to yez, am I, sir?"

"Peter, I'll tell you just how useful you are. From now on, you're in command. I hope we can catch up in time to save the deputy marshal, without getting gunned down ourselves. But those are your decisions, Sergeant."

O'Hara slowly munched another piece of jerky. "I'd be better off if I'd stayed in the cavalry, sir, but ye remember I got married about the time ye was workin' on Major Foos's case, an' a man wants more for his wife than army pay."

"I remember. A Pennsylvania teamster's daughter—Schmidt, wasn't it? Rose—Rosetta—Rosalie—what was it?"

"Rozeen, sir, the best woman that ever lived, an' I drank all that up, too."

The Foos case had happened eleven years before. O'Hara would have been in his middle thirties then. Hewitt seemed to remember the bride as being a very pretty woman with dark eyes, dark curly hair and a ripe and busty figure. He had wondered at the time how she had remained unmarried so long, because she had been at least twenty-five herself.

Or how did he know she had never married? It was always a mistake to take anything for granted, especially about good-looking women.

It plainly hurt O'Hara to talk about her, but he seemed to want to anyway. "Where is she now, do you know?" Hewitt asked.

"Off to California more than a year past, sir, wid a better man. I'll not be botherin' her again. I only want her to be happy now. Some things ye can't have back. But by God, I *can* quit the whiskey!"

"You owe yourself that much, Peter—yourself, not your wife."

O'Hara merely nodded before turning his horse and heading up the trail. Hewitt called after him, "Take care, there. Remember, this fellow is a cold-blooded, back-shooting killer."

O'Hara turned to look back, his face magically at peace, as though he had got something out of his system again, at least for the time being. "I fought the 'Paches, sir," he said. "I learned to track from a 'Pache scout. Ye could respect the 'Paches, sir. In their way they was brave sojers. Huks is as cruel as the 'Paches without bein' a brave man, but I won't let him bushwhack me."

"You've got the idea."

An hour later, O'Hara had to stop and dismount in a shaking fit. Before Hewitt could reach him, O'Hara was sitting on the ground, his teeth chattering, his face gray. He had the eyes of a beaten dog.

"I'd help if I could," Hewitt told him, "but this battle you fight alone. If you want to surrender, remember, there's a bottle in the pack."

O'Hara struggled to his feet. "We'll ride on a bit, sir. Since Rozeen left me—a year an' more now—I've lived on the whiskey. 'Tis me worst enemy—worse than the 'Paches, worse than Durango Slim—but I'm not going to be a drunk the rest of me life."

Before he could mount, Hewitt caught him by the arm. "Peter, the decentest, kindest men I ever knew were drunks like you—drunks who kicked it out the hard way, just as you're doing—drunks who learned they never could take that first harmless drink. There's no medicine that will help you, but you've got a friend. Remember that."

"Thank yez, sir."

"I said I was your *friend*. Drop that 'sir.' I'm Jeff to my friends."

"Fine, Jeff. We'll move out now. That horse of Huks's is playin' out already. Keep a sharp watch behint us. Two pairs of eyes be better than one."

By midafternoon they were well up into the pines, feeling the cold breath that came down from the eternal snows on the peaks. O'Hara knew how to get the most out of a horse without hurting it, and, from his comments, Durango Slim was not.

"His horse is walkin' cramped in the hindquarters," he reported once.

"You can read that from the tracks?"

"Yis. Ride a horse too hard on a downhill slope an' he may slip a shoulder. On a hard climb, it's the long muscles of the hindquarters that knot up and make him walk spraddle-assed. 'Tis plain to be seen, Jeff."

Not long after that, they began to see patches of snow on all sides. And shortly, O'Hara again motioned Hewitt to ride forward. He pointed to the trail. Hewitt saw the tracks of two horses, but that was all.

"He's let Huks get around him," O'Hara said.

Hewitt felt a chill deeper than that of the chill mountain breeze. "You're sure, Peter? How?"

"Whin the marshal stopped to rest his mount, like the good horseman he is, Huks flogged his'n off into the timber and passed him. Now he can pick his spot, an' God help the marshal."

Hewitt thought it over. "Huks will be thinking only of the marshal. Maybe I can get close enough to take cards in this game, without being seen."

" 'Tis the way I'd do it if I was in shape, but ye oughtn't to take chances, Jeff. This takes a man who's fought the 'Paches from the saddle."

"I'll try it anyway. My horse is in better shape than yours. You watch, in case he breaks back down the slope. All you can do is hide, so long as he's got that rifle."

"Would ye be tellin' a man that's fought the 'Paches when to hide, now?"

They grinned at each other. Hewitt pushed his horse up the well-marked trail at a fast walk, breaking into a trot when it leveled out for short distances. Soon he left the trail altogether and pulled off into the snow under the trees. He carried the Remington in his right hand, finger on the trigger, and did his best to use all the cover he could and at the same time make speed.

The snow underfoot made it hard going for the horse, but the temperature was falling rapidly up here and the slippery trail was freezing over and becoming still more treacherous. He had to stop once to rest his horse. He pushed on again, aware suddenly that although it was still early in the afternoon, the sun had already settled down behind the peaks. In the western valleys between the Sierra Nevada and the Pacific there were hours of sunlight left, but here night was falling.

Shortly he stopped again to let his horse blow. It took so long for the horse to breathe naturally that it came to him how high they had climbed and how rare the air was here.

It was just as he started the horse again that he heard it, the heavy crash of that Winchester '73 that had been fired at him this morning. There was no scream of the big slug's passage, which meant that Durango Slim was not firing at him. It was hard to judge how far ahead he was, but here the trail traversed a round, treeless but brush-covered shoulder of the mountain.

Ideal cover! He kicked the horse into a run, threading his way through the brush. Again the big gun crashed. The fact that there were no answering shots meant just one thing.

Durango Slim had killed the deputy marshal.

But now he had to swap horses, and for a few moments at least would be afoot. Hewitt pushed his tired horse farther to the left, deeper into the brush. All he could do was keep going.

When he saw the horse coming awkwardly down the slope, he threw himself from the saddle and closed his hand over his own horse's nostrils. It was a big brown gelding that was limping badly, and it looked like the horse he had seen from a distance this morning. It had neither saddle nor bridle and was a tired, lonesome horse heading for home.

It passed safely, keeping to the trail. Hewitt led his horse forward, picking his way carefully, thankful that the snow muffled their steps. The trouble was, if the brush hid him from Durango Slim, it also hid Durango Slim from him.

He did not realize that he had got around his man until he heard him swearing at the horse behind him. Hewitt quickly tied his own horse and slipped through the brush toward the sound. In a moment he dropped to his knee and carefully brought up the Remington.

I don't want to kill him, he reminded himself. I *can't* kill him. I've got to bring him back alive. . . .

The dead deputy marshal lay on his face less than a hundred and fifty yards away. Durango Slim had already swapped bridles and was now cinching his own saddle on the lawman's horse. He had no bedroll, only a small leather valise, and no camp gear. The thick sandwich he was gobbling so greedily no doubt had been part of the deputy marshal's trail rations.

Hewitt took careful aim and then lowered the .30-30. He could see the man clearly, and it was the man who had been described to him as Durango Slim both in Colorado and in Kelly's Ravine. Nimble chunk of a man, make a good middleweight fighter. Good boots, striped pants, good jacket with a wolf collar.

And a Winchester '73.

There was one chance. Hewitt held his .30-30 at the ready and shouted, "Watch for Christ's sake that he doesn't break back down the trail and get away. I'm above him and he won't come this way. Take cover and drill him if he comes back down!"

Durango Slim stood a second or two as though paralyzed. Then he scrambled into the saddle, swinging the heavy rifle in his outstretched hand. Hewitt snapped a shot close to him, close enough for Durango Slim to hear that unforgettable scream. And another.

His luck was back. His second shot plowed a raw furrow across the horse's high croup. Durango Slim could hear that one, too, not a foot behind him, but he had all he could do to stay on the crazed horse.

"Here he comes down the trail! Take your time, hit him anywhere you can, just hit him!" Hewitt shouted.

Durango Slim hauled the horse out of the deep-cut trail and plunged off up the canyon wall to the north. Hewitt fired another shot into the leaves of some early vine that had twined around the dead, white trunk of an ancient tree.

Durango Slim was out of sight, but for what seemed an eternity he was not yet out of hearing. Nothing that Hewitt had heard about him suggested that he was much of a woodsman, and O'Hara had said that he did not know the passes. Well, he was probably due for a long, miserable night on the mountain.

There was nothing to do now but wait for O'Hara—but not near the dead deputy marshal, just in case Durango Slim lost his sense of direction and came blundering back on his own trail. Hewitt felt pretty sure that O'Hara would be along before dark. He might not have heard the shouting or the noise Durango Slim's horse had made, but he would know it was Hewitt's .30-30 that had fired those three shots.

Hewitt returned to his horse and kept it company. He debated having a cigar. He had four in his jacket pocket, four more in the pack on the pack horse. Maybe O'Hara smoked. All right, he would wait.

CHAPTER IV

O'Hara showed up less than ten minutes later. The war-wise old trooper had reasoned that if anyone came back down the slope he would not use the trail. He had pushed close enough to hear Hewitt's bluffing shouts at Durango Slim, the three shots from the Remington .30-30 and Durango Slim's wildly terrified flight to the north.

"Good thinkin', Jeff," he said. "He'll end up in a blind canyon that looks like a pass, but it ain't. He'll lose a day getting back. Ye'd have made a good sojer, do ye know that?"

"I was a good soldier," said Hewitt.

O'Hara had caught Durango Slim's spent horse. It was not permanently damaged, he thought, and could make it to Sacramento without slowing them too much. He found the deputy marshal's saddle and bridle, where Durango Slim had thrown them into the brush. He studied the dead man carefully.

"Shot the first time in the guts," he decided, "to knock him from the saddle from a good bit off. 'Twould have killed him, that one, in time, but Huks couldn't wait. He shot him through the heart wid that Winchester from no more than ten feet off, I'd say."

"We'll have to bury him," said Hewitt, "but first I want to get a sketch of what he looks like."

"We'd best figger on campin' here tonight, Jeff. That

sorry bastard will never show up here again, and 'twill come on dark before we've give the poor marshal a dacent grave. We'd best make our fire an' cook us a bait, so the fire can be put out before dark. Just in case, ye know."

"All right, let's see what he has on him, and then you start digging and I'll make his picture."

The dead man would never see his thirtieth birthday. He had a plain, strong face, good teeth, brown hair newly cut; and he wore new clothing. He had no wallet on him, and only a little silver in his pockets.

Not until Hewitt turned him over on his back did he find his deputy marshal's badge, pinned to the inside of his coat. Perhaps Durango Slim had shot him down and escaped without knowing that he had murdered a federal officer. He would be driven by fresh terrors when he learned that awful truth.

O'Hara took the shovel from the pack and opened the pack enough for Hewitt to take out a small, worn, leather-covered box. From it Hewitt took a roll of rough drawing paper and his artist's crayons, a professional set. He knelt beside the dead man and, in the protracted mountain twilight, carefully made his portrait. He took pains to show the man as he surely had looked before those two .44 slugs cut him down. He gave the healthy flush of youth and life to the gray skin. He showed him with his blue eyes open, his lips parted in a slight smile over his strong, regular teeth.

Meanwhile O'Hara hacked at the frozen earth to dig a shallow grave. "I found his saddle pack," he said, coming to Hewitt's side just as the portrait was finished. "Huks tuk his ammunition but left his gun. Tuk all the food he could eat without cookin' and left everything else."

"What's there?"

"Nought but new clothes. I doubt the man was on duty. He packed like a man on a holiday."

Hewitt held up the drawing. "Is this like him?"

"Him to the life, God rest his soul," O'Hara said, crossing himself. "Build a fire now, and cook us a bait while I bury him and pile stones on the grave. For we can't take him wid us—not an' go fast. The hard climb's still ahead of us."

Hewitt found dead wood enough to build a small, hot fire. He put the coffeepot in the edge of it and the skillet full of bacon in the center. On the other side he tilted a piece of shale to catch the heat, and on it patted out some ashcakes—cornmeal, salt, water, and bacon grease.

He hung the deputy's saddle and bridle in a tree, above the reach of most varmints. By then O'Hara had the man safely buried, but he showed signs of going into another hangover shaking fit.

"In case he's of the Holy Church," O'Hara said, "can we not say a bit of a prayer? I know I'd want a Hail Mary or two, meself."

"Of course."

Halfway through the prayer, O'Hara's fit got the better of his memory, and Hewitt had to recite it. He recited it again five times, O'Hara shivering and mumbling and crossing himself clumsily. Hewitt had to lead him to the fire from the grave.

"Drink this. It'll warm you up," he said, holding a tin cup full of coffee to O'Hara's chattering teeth.

"God damn it, man, let me alone!" O'Hara snarled. "Can't ye see how I'm sufferin'? I'd only puke it up. I've got to get warm, man!"

"I'll get you warm." Hewitt spread one of their blankets

on the ground. "Take off your coat and shirt, and lie down on your belly with your arms out."

"The hell wid yez. How big a fool do ye take me for?"

Hewitt went to the pack and took out a pint bottle of excellent, aged whiskey. He knelt with it beside the Irishman.

"If all you want is to get warm, this will do it quicker than everything in the world. If you want to get well, you've got to have the guts to hurt a little. Make up your mind, you thick-headed mick."

O'Hara started to reach greedily for the bottle, but his hand fell, and he clenched both fists and looked away from it. "I told yez," he said, between chattering teeth, "I've tuk me last drink. If it's yer custom to have a nip before supper, go ahead. But for God's sake, Jeff, let me be, let me be!"

Hewitt went twenty feet away to smash the bottle over a rock, so O'Hara could not even smell its fumes. "Lie down on your belly, as I told you," he said. "That's an order. Off with your coat and shirt!"

O'Hara peeled them off and lay down, moaning in agony. Hewitt got on his knees astride O'Hara and began kneading the muscles in his neck, shoulders and back. "It's not cold that makes you shiver, Peter," he said. "It's spasms in the muscles. Know what a spasm is?"

"Yis."

"We've got to unlock them so you can relax and eat and keep it down."

"Christ, man, why not take a hatchet to me back and be done wid it?"

"Found a sore place, did I? Ah, that's a bad one!"

"Ye've got magical fingers, Jeff," O'Hara said, in a normal voice, a few minutes later. " 'Tis no longer freezin' I am, except I'd like me shirt on me."

"Let's wait a minute or two. I know where you have a few kinks left, whether you do or not."

"Where'd you learn to do this?"

"From a doctor I sent to prison for murder. He got it from a Chinese healer in Oakland."

"Ye can make good pictures, too. Rozeen wrote poems, merry little funny ones. I forget what she called them and I can remember only one of 'em. 'Twas about me, right after we was married. It went so. . . ."

He had to take a moment to control his emotions. Then he recited:

> *"A handsome young sergeant named Peter,*
> *He married a wife, and he beat her.*
> *It was just what she needed,*
> *Because she proceeded*
> *To get sweeter and sweeter and sweeter."*

"Limericks," Hewitt said.

"Ah, yis. I knew 'twas named for one of the dear counties to Ireland, but Kilkenny was all I could think of."

Hewitt stood up. O'Hara put on his shirt and coat, and helped himself to food before they let the fire die down. Hewitt was sleepy to the point of exhaustion, but O'Hara's devils would be driving him hard tonight. He *had* to talk and listen or go mad.

"How'd ye learn so many things, Jeff?"

"By doing them. The Army was my first teacher, would you believe it?"

"It was mine, too. Tell me about it, Jeff, else I'll go mad and start screamin'."

Hewitt told him how he had come out of the Ozarks as a near-illiterate boy of fifteen. How he had lied about his age to join up, being sent to the Presidio of San Francisco for basic training.

"I never left there. I was assigned to Headquarters Company as a clerk. I was a quiet one, and timid. I never envied the officers their rank and privileges, but how I envied them their education!

"I went to a secondhand bookstore and bought books—textbooks, novels, collections of sermons, and a dictionary. I set myself a task of three books a week and ten new words a day. Mathematics came easily to me, but I had to learn grammar from books, and by paying attention to how the better-educated officers talked. And I tell you, it gave me a lot of pleasure to realize how badly some of them mangled the English language."

"You went at education the way a drunk does the whiskey."

"Just about. Hold it a moment."

Hewitt picked up the .30-30 and went a little way from camp to listen. All he could hear was the peaceful foraging of their hobbled horses. He returned to the cold fire, where O'Hara listened raptly as he went on:

"The more I learned, the more ignorant I felt. I vowed to become the best company clerk in the Army, and maybe I did it. I served five years, one month and sixteen days. As you know, a good company clerk is the most valuable man in the peacetime Army. But then came the mutiny."

"At the Presidio? I never heard of it."

"It never got into records, but the captain of Headquarters Company was beaten half to death and a simpleminded shavetail who tried to rescue him got it almost as bad. The O.D. was a lieutenant colonel. That day he was so drunk he was walking into walls. He tried to order out a rifle platoon and a platoon of M.P.'s. They refused to obey, and one of them took a shot just over his head.

"He made a run for the latrine and they let him make it, but then he made the mistake of firing his forty-five at them. They all cut loose then. They didn't try to hit him, but they filled that latrine full of lead."

"I'd call that a mutiny, meself."

Hewitt went on to tell how, thirty hours later, the mutineers—now grown to more than half the company—were still barricaded in their quarters when General H. H. "Hydrophoby" Hazlit got off the train, all unsuspecting. He was an old man who had been a sergeant under Don Carlos Buell, who commissioned him in the field.

Hydrophoby relieved the colonel and the lieutenant colonel and took command himself. He called in Corporal Hugh Goff. That was the name to which Jefferson Hewitt had been born, and under which he had enlisted.

"Close the door, soldier," the general said. "When I want to know what's going on, I ask the company clerk. Be at ease, boy. Pull up a chair and sit down."

"Is that an order, sir?"

Hydrophoby glared. "No, if you put it that way, but nothing you say here will ever be traced back to you. Just tell me what the hell has gone wrong with this company. The truth, now, damn it!"

"The truth," Corporal Goff said, "is that an incompetent, cowardly, bullying captain who is not fit to drive a team of mules is in command. The lieutenant would make a good officer in time, sir, with a good C.O. But he followed the only example he had and it almost cost him his life. These are the facts, sir. Anything else would be not merely untruthful but irrelevant."

Hydrophoby glared at him, the mad-dog look that had

terrified more officers than enlisted men. Hydrophoby was what they called a soldier's soldier.

"*Irrelevant?*"

"Yes, sir. The colonel knows how incompetent the captain is. Ask him."

"Why doesn't he do something about it?"

"The colonel was forty-first in his class at West Point and the captain was sixth in his. I'm sure the general knows how important those standings are in the officer corps."

"Yes, but I didn't know that every corporal in the Army knew it. Now that you're rating your officers, tell me what kind of rate you'd give your colonel."

"It requires no great perspicuity, sir, to discern that the colonel's irresolute cunctation will always have him in a command crisis of some kind."

"Perspicuity?" Hydrophoby gurgled. "*Cunctation?*" He took a life-saving chew of cut plug and masticated it steadily into shape. "Sit down, Corporal—and this time, God damn it, that's an order."

Talking kept O'Hara from twitching, and it was good soldier talk for Hewitt, too. It recalled his youth, gave him back his perspective. The man who had talked up to Hydrophoby Hazlit and gotten away with it had no business fearing defeat by Cleve Huks, *alias* Durango Slim.

"What did the gin'ral do?" O'Hara asked.

Hewitt chuckled. "Cleaned house."

The colonel and the captain were permitted to resign their commissions. The lieutenant was assigned to a frontier company under a dedicated captain who would make a good officer of him. A week later, Hydrophoby Hazlit sent for the corporal again.

"Boy, how would you like to go to West Point?"

"Thanking the general—but no, sir."

"Why not? You're still young enough to make us a crackin' good officer."

"And old enough to know that I'm a loner, sir. The Army has taught me to know my limitations. My time will be up in two years, sir, and then I'm taking my ticket."

Hydrophoby sighed. "Well, I doubt there's a place in this man's Army for an enlisted man with your sophisticated cynicism about his officers. Know what sophisticated cynicism is, son?"

"Yes, sir. It's usually reserved for officers."

"You see, boy, you make me self-conscious about my own vocabulary and grammar."

The corporal drawled, "But ah can toke pyore hillbilly, seh, if hit'll greaze the rope that hangs me."

Hydrophoby laughed. "How would you like my personal citation, an honorable discharge, and a recommendation to a civilian job that will pay you twenty times what you make as a company clerk?"

He knew better than to refuse. He became a Pinkerton agent on the Oakland docks and helped smash an organized ring that had been robbing the warehouses blind for years. He had learned fair Spanish from two soldiers in his company and a little German and French from two more. He posed as a fugitive who had been living in Mexico and Europe, but who had had to come home when he went broke.

He was a good detective and he liked the life. He stayed with the Pinkerton agency nearly four years, working mostly criminal cases. Then a Cheyenne bank offered to back him and another man in a company to bond public and corporation officers. More than ever a loner, Hewitt hesitated to take on a stranger as a partner.

But he liked Conrad Meuse at sight. Meuse was a German immigrant, a former professor of philosophy who had got out of Germany two jumps ahead of the police. There he had been known as a radical, not just a reformer but a potential revolutionary. Deep in his heart, Conrad was a cautious conservative who had not enjoyed the university. He found his real vocation in accounting, economics and finance.

They had now been partners for years in Bankers Bonding and Indemnity Company. Conrad ran the Cheyenne office and wrote the surety bonds, meanwhile conducting a thriving investment business. Hewitt did the field work on the bonds and worked the criminal cases that were earning more and more of their money, as their reputation grew.

Today, Hewitt was a synthetic man. He had used the names of Aaron B. London, Zeke Harvey, Alec Laidlaw, Richard Bing, Reuben Whitman and Jefferson Hewitt on his cases. He assumed a different personality with each name. He had been Alec Laidlaw, a rascally horse broker from Syracuse, New York, when he met Sergeant Peter O'Hara. He had cleared a good officer, Major Horatio Foos, of trumped-up charges of embezzlement on which a conniving civilian purchasing agent had tried to frame him.

But he liked Jefferson Hewitt best of all his borrowed personalities; and so Jefferson Hewitt he had become. Hewitt was a good shot—almost as good as he was reputed to be. He had added enough Italian to his languages to carry on a conversation. He was an illustrator who might have become a real artist, had he tried to learn in time. He could have made his living at gambling, mechanics, cabinetmaking, woodcarving or anything to do with livestock. He was, as he had proved to O'Hara, an expert masseur.

He knew himself to be a jack of all trades and master of none. He was a man's man, but he liked women and women liked him. He was as much at home in New York, Philadelphia and Washington as on his own beat—which was everything west of the Missouri River.

Hewitt did not know how rich he was because Conrad Meuse kept the books, but he knew himself to be wealthy. They could both have retired. They did not because both enjoyed work and chafed at idleness. Both hated injustice —and liked money. Both could make a little money go a long way, but both liked a lot of money a lot more.

Hewitt was rarely in Cheyenne. He and Conrad always quarreled over his expense accounts and in fact could not stand each other very long at a time. Conrad wore a beard, a tiepin with a black pearl, a watch chain with rubies in it, and always a high collar and tie.

"But you, Jefferson," he said, "are a savage. You go about like a tramp at your work, stinking for a bath, needing a shave. *Ach, Gott*—why, Jefferson, why?"

"To make money for us, you bejeweled and perfumed feather duster," Hewitt replied.

They were the best of friends.

Conrad would have shunned O'Hara like a plague carrier, but Hewitt sat up with him until almost daylight, now and then getting up to prowl the icy mountainside with the .30-30. O'Hara dozed off with the blankets around him, and awakened at daylight in black depression.

"Me sleepin' dreams be worse than me wakin' ones," he said. "Ye've got to have yer own sleep, man, so git into the blankets and give me the damn gun. I'll not have it said that Peter O'Hara couldn't do his sentry go."

The sun was high in the eastern sky when Hewitt awakened to the perfume of frying bacon and bubbling coffee. O'Hara had retrieved the deputy marshal's saddle and bridle, and had put them on Durango Slim's horse. Their own horses were saddled and bridled. All that remained was to load the pack horse after they had eaten.

Again O'Hara took the lead, morose and scowling. He refused to consider the possibility that Durango Slim was ahead of them. "Do ye think I don't know the damned pass?" he snarled. "There's no other way he could git through, so he's behint us. So let be, let be!"

He was suffering not just depression but a real, physical need for the comfort of whiskey. He was still able to find them a good spot for their noon fire, in the sunlight that was all the more precious because they were now higher still, and it was colder. But after eating he began to shiver again, and Hewitt was afraid he would throw up his food.

He made the Irishman lie down for more massage. It relieved the shivering spasm quickly, but O'Hara would not stand for much of it. "Stop it now," he said. "Let's not waste the cure nor the time. I'll need it worse another day, and we must make the summit before dark."

They crossed creeks flowing with icy runoff water. In a few weeks they would be raging rivers; and in a few more, mere trickles. All around them now there was deep snow. It looked solid and dense, but it was still melting wherever the sun hit. To Hewitt it felt colder than it was because the air was so thin here. Without its usual oxygen supply, the blood seemed somehow not up to its task of warming him.

The soil under the snow grew thinner and the trees became smaller. The strange thing was that not one sound of a living thing could be heard except for their own horses. The birds were weeks away. They had left the squirrels behind. The deer would move up with the thaw and the bears were still denned up in their winter sleep.

The horses went without feed at noon and barely caught

their breath as they waited. They began panting again soon after they resumed the trail.

The early twilight came, and still they struggled on. O'Hara had not spoken a word since noon. Now, suddenly, Hewitt noticed horse tracks in the snow—many tracks of many unshod horses, like themselves westbound through the pass.

"Peter," he called.

O'Hara turned in the saddle. "Yis?"

"We have company on the trail," Hewitt said, pointing to the tracks.

"Washo Indians," O'Hara replied. "Friends of mine. Usually they're first through Carson Pass, whin they go down to the towns to do a bit of tradin'."

"What if Durango Slim finds an Indian to take him through?"

"Ye don't know him and ye don't know the Washos. Cleve wud treat an Indian like the dirt, and the Washos don't stand for that kind of abuse."

"But if he pulled a gun—"

"He'd end up in snow up to his butt, wid the Washo laughin' at him just out of Winchester range. Quit worryin'. Ye hired me to do this job—now let me do it."

"Where will we spend the night?"

"I'll worry about that, too."

O'Hara was in a savage humor and there was nothing to do but let him have his way. Shortly a frigid western breeze sprang up, coming seemingly from nowhere, but Hewitt knew that they were now close to the summit of the pass. That air movement had begun, warm and wet, in the western valleys beyond the mountains. As the pressure of its own expansion forced it up through the pass, it left its heat behind.

Hewitt never knew the exact moment they reached the watershed, but the moment came when he realized that they were now on a downhill slope that the horses liked better. Now they skated over patches like ice, or broke through a glassy crust into deep snow through which they floundered with difficulty.

Stubbornly O'Hara pushed on, holding his horse to a fast walk into the deepening shadows. Dusk came later here than it had yesterday, on the eastern slope, but it had come at last. Hewitt held his peace. He could do nothing but trust O'Hara, whether he wanted to or not.

The Irishman pulled his horse off the trail suddenly and began to climb the canyon wall. Ahead of him, Hewitt saw the tracks of the unshod Washo horses. The darkness fell suddenly, but still O'Hara rode on. Now he began to sing raucously:

> "'Sojer, sojer, won't you marry me?'
> 'Oh no, no, no, not I,
> For how can I marry such a pretty girl as you
> When I have no coat to put on?'
> Then away she went to the coater-oater shop,
> An' she bought him one
> Of the very, very best,
> An' the sojer put it on."

Two broad, bulky men materialized out of the darkness, one carrying a Remington .30-30, identical to Hewitt's, in his hands. "Jeff," said O'Hara, "meet me friend Lord Cecil McTigue, chief of the Washos. The two of yez should get on well. Ye'r both scamps."

CHAPTER V

Under an immense overhang of rock was, not just a room, but truly a hall, that had been protected from the snow all winter. In it were five Washo men and their six horses. There was plenty of space for Hewitt, O'Hara and their four horses. The Indians had already built a big fire, which made Hewitt uneasy.

But O'Hara said, "I've made many a camp here, Jeff, and there's no light shows from the trail. Ye have to know it's here to find it, and Durango Slim never will."

The Irishman was in an almost elated mood and he was clearly among friends. He broke out their supplies and prepared an enormous supper—canned corned beef warmed by the fire, more ashcakes and bacon, and a full pot of black, potent coffee.

"'Tis indecent for a chief not to be a lord," he said, jovially, "but he should have a good Irish name, too. I've adopted Lord Cecil into me own County Sligo tribe."

The Washos had naturally grave faces, but their quick, small smiles and dark, twinkling eyes easily expressed both humor and affection. Any friend of O'Hara's, their attitude said, was a friend of the Washos.

"But Cecil's a distinguished English name," Hewitt said, joining into the spirit of the evening. "The first Cecil was Queen Elizabeth's chancellor, really the first Prime Minister of the Empire."

"Oh, the hell ye say!"

"I'm sure of it, Peter."

"Be damned! I grew up wid a boy be the name of Cecil McTigue, so I thought 'twas a good Irish name. Well, no matter. Did ye ever see anyone look more Irish than the chief?"

Hewitt was not sure how much the Washos understood of all this, but they enjoyed it. Yet, ten minutes later, the hilarity went out of the evening. One of the Washos muttered something in his own language to O'Hara, who shook his head and said, "No, no, no." The Washo argued. O'Hara snapped at him irritably and then appealed to Lord Cecil.

"I'm off the stuff, Lord Cecil," he said, "an' it'll be a sad day for the Washos if ye go on drinkin' it. We've nary a drop wid us—tell the bastard that."

Lord Cecil did not seem pleased. No doubt he had looked forward to helping drink up O'Hara's trail whiskey; no doubt they had done so in the past. O'Hara had no right to swear off in their behalf, nor was it quite a friendly act to swear off himself.

But when O'Hara opened their pack completely, and proved that they had not a drop of whiskey with them, the Indians accepted it philosophically. After they had eaten, they were cheerful again in their grave and slightly derisive way. Hewitt had never met Washos before, and he liked them immediately.

Hewitt broke out one more of his last few cigars, and lighted it. They passed it solemnly from hand to hand, but O'Hara had descended again into despondency and would not even smoke with them. He was as restless as a caged cat and, Hewitt thought, ready to pick a quarrel with anyone.

"Peter," Hewitt said. O'Hara did not seem to hear him. Hewitt raised his voice. "Peter!"

"What now?"

"I've heard that the second day is the worst. If—"

"Then ye heard wrong," O'Hara said savagely. "I've been foine today, and do ye know why?"

"Because you've kept busy."

"Oh yis, that helps. But mostly 'tis because I've got a friend. I never had one. Many's the man I trusted behint me in a skirmish wid the hostiles or to get drunk wid after, or lie for him to the captain, or him for me. But not a friend, do ye know what I mean?"

"I think so. How about a treatment to break up the knots in your back muscles?"

"I think not now, but if I have me a bad night, ye can try then. Fer now, just talk to me. Help me keep me mind off me guilt."

"What guilt?"

The Indians were listening silently. Again Hewitt was not sure how much they understood; quite a bit would be his guess.

"Rozeen," said O'Hara, "an' what I done to make her leave me for a better man. Sold a four-mule span of mine in Reno, she did, an' the harness wid 'em. But 'twas the least she was entitled to, poor dear, an' I hope she's happy now."

"Haven't you heard whether she is or not?"

"No word, but if she had the spirit to sell me best mules and run off, she'll make herself a new life, don't you figger?"

"That's probably true, but how long are you going to drag your guilt around like a tin can tied to the tail of a dog? Life goes on. It had to go on for her. It has to go on for you. Was he a good man?"

"She'd have no other. I didn't know him, but he'd be all that I wasn't. Dacent. Sober, kind—you know!"

"Did you never meet him?"

"No. Bob Stanley's his name, a surveyor for the railroad builders, I heard, down on his luck because he'd been sick a year. A one-eyed man wid a patch over it. A neat, clean man in a black suit an' derby hat to his head, very quiet-spoken an' always the gentleman. Why shud I wish them annything but good luck that they fell in love?"

"You're a better man than I could be."

"God, I'm the world's worst, Jeff! Talk to me or I'll go crazy."

"What about?"

"Why are we afther chasin' Cleve Huks? What did he do?"

Hewitt said slowly, "That's not easy for me to talk about. Like you with Rozeen, I'm carrying a load of guilt myself. I could have prevented it, and now I'm not sure I can even bring him to justice. This case could be the worst failure of my life."

"What did he do?"

"Murder."

"I guessed that. Who did he murther?"

"A very nice, very pretty girl, only fifteen years old, one who had no father or brothers to protect her."

"And ye think ye shud have?"

"Someone should have. I could have, I think."

"What'll ye do when he's in yer grip—shoot him down, or put him in cuffs?"

"Neither. First I have to prove that he did it, or I can't touch him. Peter, we can't even prove that he killed the young deputy marshal. He won't show up in Sacramento with the marshal's horse. He'll get rid of it somewhere and buy another fair and square, and no court in the country would convict him on our testimony."

"Then I say the hell wid the courts! I know friends in Sacramento who'll hang him higher than a bird can fly, if I but give the word."

"Oh no! He has to be extradited to Colorado, stand trial, be convicted and hang."

"Or ye don't get paid."

"No, I'm being paid handsomely, and if you stay with me until the job is done, I'll see that you're paid more than you ever earned in your life."

"No, I don't want pay, only me food. Maybe it'll make up in me heart for what I done to Rozeen."

"This is business, Peter. You're the man I need."

"But what if I go off on a bit of a toot?"

"You won't."

"Tell me about it, Jeff," O'Hara pleaded. "If I know how bad it is, maybe I'll fergit the job still to be done in case somebody offers me a drink. A man's got to have more than good sense to kick the whiskey. He needs a bed of coals in him."

Hewitt still was not sure how much the Washos understood, but somehow they were a comfort as well as his judges. When you came right down to it, a man was his own judge. Perhaps even more than O'Hara, he needed to hear his own voice say the things he had left unsaid through all this endless, despairing chase across four states.

"Did you ever hear of Simon C. Rankin, Peter?"

"The Powder River man what owns the Dot Seven Bar? The ould troop camped a month on his place once."

"He's more than a cattleman. He's a wealthy lawyer with offices in Cheyenne and Washington. I've known him for

twenty years. We've done some work for him over all those
years, on his cases. I've known his daughter, Emma, since
she herself was fifteen."

Emma Rankin had been as headstrong as she was smart
and pretty. He could remember—could indeed never forget
—the evening when he had come so close to violating his
friendship with her father, on that very Powder River ranch
that O'Hara knew.

"*I want you to be my first, Jeff. Oh, don't be so stuffy!
Dr. Landre says—*"

"*I don't give a damn what Landre says. He—*"

"*You should. He wanted to be my first. I wish you could
talk to him. He's got different ideas than anyone on earth.
He believes in being free to—*"

"*There's nothing new or different about his ideas, Emma.
He—God damn it, keep your hands to yourself or I'm
going to paddle you.*"

"*I dare you to. I dare you!*"

Dr. Jacques Landre had spent a year in Wyoming, getting over a heart attack—or so he said. Hewitt had wondered from the first what a rich, distinguished French phy-
sician was doing, buried away in the West all that time.
Probably another underage girl in Paris.

Landre was forty-five, bald, potbellied, popeyed, but as
Gallic as the guillotine with woman. Emma insisted on telling Hewitt about Landre's "freedom" philosophy, and she
made it sound reasonable, all right. But his nerve held. He
made it safely back to Chyenne and, luckily, was out on another investigation when Simon and his daughter left the
ranch and came through on their way to Washington.

The moment they got back to Cheyenne the next spring,
Emma ran off with Billy Baldwin, a disbarred lawyer who
was working for a Cheyenne mortgage company as an

appraiser. He made good money and lacked Landre's compelling viciousness. Unfortunately he already had a wife and four children.

Si Rankin did not catch up with Emma for another year and a half. "Actually," Hewitt said, "she caught up with Si. She telegraphed him in Washington, from Denver, asking for money. Said she had a baby and was broke. I was in Arizona Territory then. He wired me to look into it, and he wired her a couple of hundred dollars.

"I was a month getting there. Her money was already gone. She wanted me to take the baby back to Si to raise. It was a hell of an argument. She made no bones about it. She was going to work in a sporting house."

"By God, no!"

"By God, yes. But that wasn't the limit of her ambition. She just wanted to learn the business and open a house of her own. Baldwin, poor devil, had been kicked to death by a horse. She made a good case for herself—no husband, no longer a right to wear her father's name, no future, no reputation—why not go into such a profitable business? What did she have to lose?"

Rather than tell Si the truth, he wired Conrad Meuse for money. Bankers Bonding and Indemnity Company supported Emma and her baby while Hewitt tried to reason with the woman.

"Finally I got an idea. There was a dry-goods store that could be bought cheaply, and she had her father's eye for a dollar. She agreed that she could make more money in it than she could running a sporting house."

BB&I bought the store for her and advanced the money needed for new fixtures and stock. Hewitt and Meuse had over $6,000 in it before they thought it wise to tell Simon C. Rankin about it. Meuse told him in Cheyenne. Rankin started at once for Denver. Meuse wired Hewitt that he was on the way, and Hewitt tried to prepare Emma to be at least kind to her father.

"*All right, but he's not going to tell me what to do. You're going to stay here with me, aren't you? You don't have to marry me. But you want me, don't you? And you're the man I need. Billy let me boss him around.*"

"*Let's understand each other, Emma. You're a matchless woman, but you're not for me. I'm not a marrying man and—*"

"*I told you, you don't have to marry me. And put that damned stinking cigar out and listen to me.*"

"*I would rather smoke, and I don't give a tinker's damn about the dry-goods business.*"

"*You're avoiding the issue.*"

"*Which is?*"

"*That we'd be so good together.*"

"*I think I still prefer a good cigar, Emma.*"

"*If you ever change your mind, just knock at my door, you son of a bitch, and see what happens. And you can tell my dad to go to hell, too. . . .*"

Yes sir, she was a money-maker, like old Si. Over the years she became wealthy from the store. She bought a house, a top-buggy and a good team. She kept servants and had a succession of men friends that were a rather romantic scandal in Denver. It was hard to hate Emma. What would have been wretched vice in many another woman was just naughtiness in her.

Simon C. Rankin let her alone, but he paid BB&I to have Hewitt check up on her periodically. They remained friends. He stayed at a hotel in Denver, dressed in his best to take her out to dinner and took notes as she chatted about the baby. Emma knew he was reporting to her father and did not resent it. She was hotheaded, but not mean.

Last fall he had been winding up a case in Nebraska when he got a wire from Si, from Denver:

COME MOST URGENT COLLIE IN TROUBLE

That was all. "Collie" was their code name for Emma and the problem she represented. Hewitt was in Denver thirty-six hours later. He did not look up Emma, and he had trouble finding Si, who had registered in a cheap hotel under a false name. Si had aged badly—was aging daily before Hewitt's very eyes.

Emma, he said, was having an open, scandalous affair with a worthless gambler ten years her junior. What bothered Si most was that his granddaughter was being neglected. Hewitt had not seen "the baby" for ten years, and it was hard to realize that she was now fifteen. Now Si wanted her, and Emma would not give her up.

"She tried to get into your bed once, at the ranch, didn't she?" Si snarled at Hewitt.

"Yes, she did." No point in lying now.

"God damn it, why didn't you? You could have handled her. Maybe you still can. I've got a United States Supreme Court hearing coming up, and I want you to straighten out this mess so I can concentrate on it."

"Si, what can I do? Emma is—how old is she now? Thirty-two, thirty-three—"

"Thirty-three. You can kill the son of a bitch if that's what it takes. They wouldn't prosecute you. Be more likely to strike a medal in your honor. If I were twenty years younger, I'd go after him myself."

"Who is the man?"

"Only name anybody knows for him is Durango Slim.

Works in the public stable and lives in a room over it, and makes his money playing poker at night. Beds Emma down in her own house a couple of nights a week, and by Christ, Jeff, my granddaughter is in that house! If ever a man needed killing, it's this Durango Slim."

"Come on, Si, you know better than that. Probably the best course is to prove she's an unfit mother in court and take the child away with you. No problem about that, if what you tell me is true."

"Fix it up. Do something! I'm not thinking straight, so you've got to. Whatever it costs, it's in your hands, Jeff."

Rankin left for Washington that day. Hewitt moved into the room he had vacated and hired a local private detective he had used before, Dan Holdridge. Dan already knew a lot about Durango Slim, none of it favorable. A day's quiet prowling brought in few facts but far too much disreputable rumor.

"Jeff," Dan reported, "this is a bad one. Don't know his real name, but he claims to have been a Texas Ranger and that's a damn lie. Fancy dresser, built like a fighter, an eye like a dead fish. Now, here's what gets me. He plays winning poker—nobody with any sense will play with him any more because he's as crooked as he is slick—but he's not getting rich in dime-limit games in the livery stable.

"And he's sporting too much money! He carries a wad of bills like the end of a wagon tongue and he just dares anybody to try to take it away from him. He packs a two-edged knife and a forty-four. He's damn good with the knife. Only so-so with the Colt, I think, but you know nobody's going to get into a quarrel over a poker table with a blade artist. And with a rifle, he's unbeatable."

Emma still used Billy Baldwin's name, and as far as

Denver was concerned, she was his widow. "Do you think he beat Mrs. Baldwin out of the money?" Hewitt asked.

"The man don't live who could beat her out of a dime, no matter how crazy she was about him—and she's crazy about Durango Slim, all right. There's absolutely no way you can get hold of the handle on Durango Slim. You better start with Mrs. Baldwin."

"It won't do any good," said Hewitt, "but I'll try."

Emma had never looked prettier. She had him to the house and served him a delicious supper. He met Virginia, who was prettier than her mother had been at the same age and, he thought, just as smart. But where Emma had been lively and brash, Virginia was the quiet type. Maybe a little too quiet, Hewitt thought.

"Keep an eye on him," he told Holdridge afterward. "I want to know everything he does, who he sees, where he goes. Don't try to mix with him! When it comes time for that, I'll do it."

"Jeff, he'll kill you. Durango Slim is no saloon bum. He knows he'll have to kill somebody sometime, the way he lives, and he's ready for it."

"He can try. I'd like to sit in on a game with him. You find out how—when—where. . . ."

CHAPTER VI

There was no game that night, or the next, or any night after that. It took a lot of scouting for Dan to determine that Durango Slim had been seen riding southward on the Durango road. His flashy sorrel horse could not be mistaken. Neither could the alligator-hide valise he had tied on behind the saddle.

"He must've left," Dan reported, "before noon, and he cleaned out that boar's nest he lived in over the stable. Maybe Mrs. Baldwin talked about you to him. Maybe he's scared off."

Somehow, Hewitt doubted that.

Emma Baldwin did not miss Virginia until the next morning, nearly twenty-four hours later. Sometimes the girl stayed overnight with a friend in the next block. What threw Emma into sudden panic was the discovery that her own team and buggy had been missing since yesterday, too.

She came at once to the hotel where Hewitt was staying.

"Jeff," she said, "I'm scared stiff. Slim didn't take that team—*she* did. They're the best. But they didn't mean anything to her. She never enjoyed driving. Where would she go?"

"Wherever he wanted her to go."

"Oh, that's nonsense! He never paid any attention to her and she was completely indifferent to him. Don't make something out of nothing, now. Why, he's fifteen years older than Virginia! He's *twice* her age."

"And Billy Baldwin was twenty years older than you when you ran off with him."

She tottered to her feet. "Oh, Christ, Jeff, you can't really believe . . ."

She choked up. He said, "I sure can, and so can you. What's his real name? Where does he come from? Where did he make that wad of money he carries?"

Emma had no answers. But she did know a man who would lend Hewitt a good saddle horse. He was on the trail to Durango an hour later.

He found the buggy some twenty miles from Denver. The team had been run to death and then turned loose. The tracks had showed clearly that another horse had been tied behind the buggy. Durango Slim's sorrel, or still another horse? Certainly it could not be Virginia's, and there was no sign of the girl near the abandoned buggy.

Nothing to do but push on. It was blind riding for a day or two, but he picked up a little sign here and there of *two* shod horses. And then he met a sheepman who had sold a pair of saddle horses to a man answering Durango Slim's description. Slim had traded in his sorrel, which had been "run into the ground," the sheepman said. No, he had not seen a girl or a second horse.

But not far away, Hewitt found the other horse, dead. The wind had almost erased all tracks, but he also found what he thought were the shadowy remains of tracks made by another pair of boots—smaller than Slim's, with flat heels. They could have been the fine button shoes that Emma said her daughter had been wearing.

Push on. What else could he do?

In Pueblo he found Virginia, too late. Someone had

found her half beaten to death not far from the main wagon road from the north. A doctor and his wife had taken her in and were doing their best for her, but she died the day Hewitt arrived without ever regaining consciousness.

Hewitt had the doctor embalm the body and bury it. He wired Si at some length, but did not wait for a reply. "Durango Slim" could have come from either Durango, Mexico, or Durango, Colorado. Hewitt had a hunch that the likes of this one would never have ventured into Mexico. The quickest way to get to Durango, Colorado, was to ride.

It was the hardest week's ride he had ever taken, but it paid off. No one there knew Durango Slim's name, but they knew him as a professional gambler who came and went, came and went. He dressed well and rode good horses, but did not care where he slept, so long as it gave him privacy. This time he had spent three days resting up in what was little more than a shed on the edge of town.

Hewitt looked it over carefully—and found nothing. Durango Slim had told someone that he was going to collect some money in Utah and then maybe "take a look at a deal in California." One thing was sure—he had ridden out of Durango on a fine horse, a brawny gray stallion for which he had peeled off twenty-five ten-dollar bills.

Hewitt returned to Denver. Emma was in a coma in the hospital. Si had just come back from Pueblo. He had shown Virginia's picture to the doctor who had attended Virginia's deathbed, and had identified her positively. He had decided to leave her buried there and help Emma pick up the pieces of her life.

"I'll take her back to Cheyenne with me," he said, "and you go after this son of a bitch and bring him back here.

Bring back the proof. Bring back what I need to prosecute him. I want to do it legally if I can. I want to be there when he hangs, and I don't care what it costs."

"The best thing," Hewitt said, "is to put out printed dodgeroos on him. Offer a reward. Someone will turn him in if you offer enough."

"And then what?" Si demanded, harshly. "What proof have we got? Not enough to extradite him. Remember this, Jeff—*nobody saw them together!* All you saw was their tracks, and a private detective is a hell of a poor witness in a hanging case. Jurymen don't like private detectives because it's their job to convict, and some of 'em don't care how they do it."

Hewitt prowled the room that Durango Slim had occupied above the livery stable. Nothing there, but in the pile of trash behind the stable, which he spent half a day sorting, he found a one-page letter. No envelope to show where it came from, but it started "Dear Slim," and it said:

Well finally I see my way clear to pay on that $2,800 I owe you. Every cent I have got is tied up in a saloon I have bought here, it's the Acey-Deucey and something has turned up in the old game that makes it just as rich as goose gravy. It's more than I can run by myself and I will give you a 50% share for the $2,800 and we will each clear $5,000 the first year. Now Slim you know I know how to run a saloon and this one is in your line, and I don't think I need to say any more except that YOU WILL KNOW WHO the man is who runs things here. So the sooner you get here, the better.

Your old buddy, Jack.

The man wrote a good hand and plainly had at least a little education. Many a saloon was called "Acey-Deucey";

Hewitt could remember three or four that he had seen himself.

He did not show the letter to Si Rankin. He might have pulled out of the job, except that Si asked him to go with him to see Emma at the hospital. Somehow Hewitt's voice got through the deathlike trance in which she was slowly wasting away, and she came suddenly awake. She was too weak and spent to make a sound, but she formed the words with her lips: "Get him."

"I'll try," Hewitt said, "if you'll do something for me. Will you do it?"

Her enormous eyes stared up at him out of her gaunt and wasted face, to ask him what he wanted done. "I'll go after him," Hewitt said, gently, "if you'll do as your father says. Eat! Get your strength back! Go back to Cheyenne with him."

Silently she said, "No, no, no."

"All right, then," he said, "if you won't try, I won't either. This is how you got into this, Emma—by doing as you damn please no matter who got hurt by it. Si will stay here until you're ready to travel. Unless you tell me you'll go back and do as he says, the hell with it, I've got more important things to do."

She promised.

His best lead—better even than the letter from "Jack"— was the fine gray studhorse Durango Slim had bought and the "deal" he wanted to "take a look at" in California. Hewitt took the train west. When he left the rails he spent Si's money freely buying two fine saddle horses and a pack mule. He headed for Utah, riding hard, making as much time as he could.

He had luck here and there; the gray horse was not hard to trace. In the Paiute country he found a "white Indian,"

married to a Paiute woman, who had had trouble with
Durango Slim. The gray horse was about spent, and the
squaw man had a fine big brown gelding he was willing to
swap if enough boot could be had.

Durango Slim handed over twenty more ten-dollar bills
and the gray horse, and put his saddle and valise on the
brown gelding. He had a gallon army canteen, too. As he
was snugging up the saddle cinch, he tossed the canteen to
one of the squaw man's kids.

"Here, go fill this for me, and hurry up about it," he said.

"You go straight to the devil," the kid said. "Who you
think you're talking to, anyway?"

"Why, you little halfbreed bastard—"

Durango Slim started to take a swipe at the kid. He
found himself looking down the barrel of the squaw man's
old .44.

"Ride!" was all the squaw man said.

"Well, hell, sorry I talked that way, but I can't ride without no drinking water."

The squaw man merely jabbed him with the muzzle of
the gun. Durango Slim tried once more.

"Listen, mister, I said I'm sorry. I been on the trail a
long time, see? I had a lot of worries, see? My old mother is
dying, and I want to get there, and my nerves is shot all to
hell."

"Your ass will be shot to hell if you ain't out of here in
fifteen seconds."

The squaw man started counting. Durango Slim
mounted up, settling his leg over the big Winchester '73
that he carried slung to the left side of the horse. One last
look in the "white Indian's" implacable eyes, and he rode.

"He took a couple of shots at me with that damn rifle,"
the man told Hewitt, "when he was out of pistol range. But

I knowed that was what he'd do, and I knowed he sure wouldn't come back to try it again."

Durango Slim had crossed the Colorado while the water was low. The early runoff had started by the time Hewitt reached the river. It was rising, silty, and as turbulent as sea under the typhoon.

And something had happened to Hewitt, too. He had not been sleeping well. He had eaten as sparsely as an Indian in famine time. He kept seeing Emma Baldwin's death mask of a face—when, that is, he was not seeing the brutally beaten face of her dying daughter. So young to die at all, and so undeserving of the hell that Durango Slim had visited on her.

"I was in too much of a hurry, Peter. Patience is one thing you learn early in this game, but I had forgotten it."

"Well, now he's behint us. But what if ye can't prove he done it?"

"One way or another, I'll do it. That's the way I make my living. There's one thing you may be able to help me with. I want to sketch a portrait of him and I've never seen the man that close. Can you describe him as I draw? Can you see his face clearly in your mind's eye?"

"Like he was standin' before us."

The Indians gathered around, muttering softly, marveling, as the picture grew by firelight. Hewitt burned page after page; O'Hara's vision of Durango Slim was vivid and clear and he would settle for no less than what he saw.

What emerged at last was a loutish man of dim-witted arrogance. There was ignorance in that face, overbearing vanity, sneering contempt, and the cruelty of a coward whose primal cowardice was probably his most important characteristic. Hewitt had met this man's kind before—and the strange thing was how powerfully such men appealed to some women.

"That's him," O'Hara said. "That's Cleve Huks."

"Does he always have this—this sort of sneering look? See what I mean, Peter? What would he look like with a more pleasant expression?"

"I don't know. I never seen him any way but this. There's one way I cud've helped ye, though. The Acey-Deucey, in Sacramento. I've been there meself."

"I heard there was such a place, and he had said something about trying California. It was the best lead I had."

"'Twas a good one. 'Tis run by a man called Jack Purefoy. He's owned it . . . let's see, the year now—an' ye said the letter was signed 'Jack.'"

"I told you, Peter, you're my luck."

"'Tis a good feelin' to be useful, Jeff. I'll turn in now. If I don't sleep, I'll ask ye to punch up me back a bit. But I think I can this night. I'll say me beads for the poor dead girl an' stop feelin' sorry for meself, an' sleep."

Hewitt remained awake long after the others had gone to sleep. No use trying to tell himself that he was not responsible personally. What a hell of a word that was, *personally!* When the world let things like this happen, every human being on earth was responsible. . . .

. . . At age fifteen, Emma had spoken no word of French. She had to ask Hewitt what *Les Fleurs du Mal* meant, and what Jacques Landre was trying to tell her when he promised her a *nouveau frisson*.

The breeze through the pass worked itself into a miniature gale. Little of it penetrated to the shelter under the shale overhang, but he could hear it whistle through the trees and brush outside, and now and then the fire swirled as though stirred by its fingers.

"*Beats me, Emma. Sometime I'll have to look it up and let you know.*"

"*Don't mention it to Daddy. He thinks Jacques is a nice man—and he isn't, he isn't!*"

"*You're right enough there.*"

"*Neither are you, but, God, how I hate nice men! You know where I want us to be when you tell me what those words mean? Guess!*"

Poor spoiled, stupid, willful girl, it had remained for that peerless *fleur du mal* Durango Slim to give her the *nouveau frisson* of her life—her last one. Well, Hewitt thought, I'll live to see that particular flower of evil blooming on a gallows tree, and that'll be new thrill enough for me. . . .

But what of Dr. Jacques Landre, corrupter of fifteen-year-old girls in their own homes? Or could you convict the poet, Charles Baudelaire, as well? On the other hand, who corrupted him?

A detective was not God, and sin was not his business. All Hewitt had to do was catch up with Cleve Huks, *alias* Durango Slim, get enough on him to extradite him to Colorado and convict him there. Not necessarily an easy job, but more his size than sitting in judgment on the world. Hewitt rolled up in his blanket between O'Hara and one of the Washos and slept like a baby. They had to stir him out when morning came.

CHAPTER VII

They rode into Sacramento about midday, two days ahead of the schedule Hewitt had set himself. The Washos had come as far as Angels Camp. They would keep an eye out for Durango Slim but would not interfere with him.

O'Hara looked almost as gaunt as Hewitt, and both were savage, silent men, O'Hara pursued by thirst and Hewitt by memories. O'Hara had said that the sheriff was not to be trusted but that the chief of police was a good man. Hewitt was willing to trust his judgment; but first they had to seek out the United States marshal.

They put the horses in a public stable and checked into a workingmen's hotel that O'Hara had used before. Hewitt had not seen Sacramento in seven or eight years, and its size and brawling, busy hustle amazed him. Their hotel was near the river front, where a steamboat was unloading a shipment for a wholesale grocer. It had brought fifty passengers. It would take back only three or four when it returned loaded with the new lumber from the enormous stacks along the river front.

Holding pens were jammed with cattle being moved up from the warm winter valleys toward the grass that would come up as the snow retreated up the mountain with the spring. Cowboys and lumbermen jammed the saloons and cafés. Hewitt let O'Hara lead the way to the marshal's office, not far from the State Capitol.

Ed Parry was gray-haired, but he was still a tough man and he had the intelligence as well as the easy smile of a successful politician. Any man useful enough to the politicians to be worth appointing usually made a damned good law officer.

Hewitt did not have to introduce O'Hara. "I lost everything, fording the Colorado," he said, "but if you want to go down to the telegraph station with me, I think I can convince you of my identity."

"Later," the marshal said. "I've heard of your firm. What's your business with me?"

Hewitt unrolled the crayon portrait he had made of the dead deputy marshal. "Know this man?"

"Sure, that's Joe Crandal, Phoenix. Hear he's been transferred to San Francisco and going to get married. What about him? Mighty good likeness of him."

Hewitt told him about Joe Crandal's death. He showed Parry the drawing, too, that he had made of Cleve Huks, *alias* Durango Slim.

"Your word against his," Parry said, handing the picture back. "Too bad O'Hara wasn't a witness, too."

"I want him for another killing that no one can prove—yet. That's my job, to get the evidence to extradite and convict him."

"How do you plan to do that?"

"If I knew, I'd sleep better. I don't think there is any use arresting him or even questioning him. I wish he could be kept under observation, but otherwise left alone."

"First we'll have to bring Joe's body down here. Wire Phoenix and San Francisco and Washington what happened. We can talk about it as we bring the body down, Mr. Hewitt."

"I'd be no help. Peter can. He's on my payroll and it won't cost the government a cent."

Parry looked at O'Hara. "Last time I saw you, you couldn't have found your butt with both hands."

"That's all behint me. I'll never take no more drinks in all me life," O'Hara growled.

"Chief Fox won't be glad to see you back here, Peter, after all the trouble you've caused. I'll do you both a favor if I take Mr. Hewitt up on his offer. All right, I'll leave at daybreak tomorrow. You be ready. I'll provide the horses and whatever else I think we need. Now, what are we going to do about Chief Fox and the sheriff?"

O'Hara hesitated to offer an opinion. Hewitt said, "I'll leave that to your judgment, but Peter thinks that Chief Fox is a good man. Maybe we ought not to keep secrets from him. Peter's not so keen on your sheriff."

Parry thought it over a moment. "This is a wide-open town, Mr. Hewitt, but Zeno Fox is an honest policeman. He's rich enough, he can afford to be honest. I won't say that Ernie Goodin, the sheriff, is *dis*honest. But just don't expect too much from him. Suppose I have Zeno look you up kinda quietly?"

Hewitt stood up. "Suits me. Now let's take that walk down to the telegraph station. You can keep those two drawings."

"I'll do that, never fear."

Marshal Parry rolled the two portraits up and locked them in a cabinet and walked with Hewitt and O'Hara down to the railroad station. The agent found two telegrams addressed to Hewitt, but he refused to hand them over.

"There's supposed to be a password," he said. "Unless you've got it, I can't give you the wires."

Bankers Bonding and Indemnity Company's telegraph bills were huge, but time was so important in this business that Conrad Meuse used the wires as freely as Hewitt. Hewitt knew how to dramatize as well as tip generously, the first time he did business with a telegrapher. If the wiremen were his friends, it could make the difference between success and failure.

"Let's see, this is April," he said, putting three silver dollars on the counter. "How about 'tumblebug' for a password—will that do?"

The agent pocketed the coins and handed over the wires. The first one, filed two weeks ago, said:

COLLIE VERY ILL STOP SIMON DEMANDS ACTION
SOONEST STOP BRINGS ME REPORT SUSPECT HEADED
TEXAS STOP AM WIRING YOU FIVE THOUSAND CARE
SACRAMENTO SPECIE BANK BUT ADVISE YOU CONSIDER
TEXAS STOP SIMON SURE OF HIS FACTS

An advance expense payment of five thousand dollars was something new. Si Rankin must be frantic, poor devil, and poor Conrad would be catching hell from him. The second wire, filed three days ago, said:

COLLIE DIED LAST NIGHT STOP SIMON INSISTS
YOU GO FT WORTH IMMEDIATELY STOP SEE HIS
COUSIN TAYLOR H DEVLIN THERE STOP NEED NOT
SAY HOW URGENT THIS IS

Hewitt's hand shook as he folded the telegram. He could see Emma's face clearly, but it was the face of a girl of fifteen, not the stricken witch whose eyes had burned at him from the hospital bed in Denver.

In his heart, he supposed, he had known this would happen. Emma had not wanted to live. Now old Si was alone in the world, and he would not want to live long either. Just long enough, probably, to see Durango Slim kicking it out at the end of a rope.

Hewitt composed himself enough to write a reply to Conrad:

GIVE SIMON MY SYMPATHY BUT TELL HIM FORGET
TEXAS STOP SUSPECT POSITIVELY IDENTIFIED
HERE STOP TELL HIM I DEMAND HIS PATIENCE
FOR THREE WEEKS STOP TELL HIM THIS IS MY
CASE TOO NOT JUST HIS STOP TELL HIM I DID
NOT FIGHT IT THIS FAR JUST TO LOSE IT

He knew that Parry was curious about the three wires. He would not be much of a policeman if he could not get at the agent's copies. Hewitt handed them over silently and Parry read them in silence.

"Don't suppose 'Simon' would be Simon C. Rankin, of Cheyenne, would he?" he said, handing back the papers.

"Yes, do you know him?"

"No, but I know men who do. He could have gone to the President for help if he had to. He went to you."

"I've known him for years. We have done other work for him on his law cases. 'Collie' is our code word for his daughter."

"The wild one."

"The only one's he's got. Or rather, had."

Parry did not bother to say that he accepted Hewitt now for what he claimed to be, but his expression showed it. "I'll tell you one thing, Mr. Hewitt," he said, "and it's a damn good thing to remember in a case like this. Private vengeance and public justice are not the same, and you can make some bad mistakes in that regard if you let yourself get confused. I'd tell Simon C. Rankin the same thing to his face."

A good man, this Parry. They shook hands, and Hewitt and O'Hara returned to their hotel. The sights and sounds of the city, and above all the smells that came out of the saloons they passed, were having their effect on O'Hara. What he could stand with only discomfort in the high passes could be agony here.

"Take off your shirt and lie down on the bed, Peter," Hewitt said, when they were up in their room. "We're going to untie a few knots in you, and then you're going to take me on a tour of Sacramento."

A spasm of murderous rage glinted briefly in O'Hara's eyes. It died. "Jeff," he whimpered, "I've freed meself of Rozeen. Why am I not free of the drink?"

"You're not free of Rozeen," Hewitt replied. "You'll never forget her, I guess. When you face up to that, maybe you won't need to drink."

Later, they walked about Sacramento together, the Irishman more at peace with himself. He led Hewitt past the Acey-Deucey. O'Hara said it had been repainted and had a new sidewalk. It stood on a corner, and on the side street a discreet doorway led up to the upper floor.

"There's another way up from inside the saloon," he said. "Used to be a sportin' house upstairs. I see they've fixed it up, too. Look to the new red curtains, Jeff, and the flower boxes on the window sills."

And now Hewitt knew why the Acey-Deucey was "just rich as goose gravy" and why Jack Purefoy had written that it was "in your line" to Durango Slim. What had only been a hunch before was now a certainty. He knew why Durango Slim always had so much money on him and why

he had tried to take Virginia Baldwin with him whether she
wanted to go or not.

At the Sacramento Specie Bank, the president himself
waited on them. "I suppose you're Mr. Hewitt or you
wouldn't know about this," he said, "but I'm still going to
have a password from you."

" 'Devouring Time, blunt thou the lion's paws,' " said
Hewitt.

"I'll be goddamned! What's it mean?"

It never hurt to shake them up a little. "It's the opening
line of Shakespeare's nineteenth sonnet. Not an easy code
to break, wouldn't you say?"

He drew one thousand dollars in cash and left the rest on
deposit, taking time to make friends with the president.
Archie Chancellor was not yet forty, young to be running a
big, busy, growing bank. Hewitt thought he could have run
anything he put his hand to. Chancellor walked around the
corner with them to the store where he bought his own
clothing, and introduced them.

Hewitt bought a black coat, gray trousers, underwear,
white shirts, boots, and a wide-brimmed black hat. On
some jobs he liked to show a bit of style, and this was one
such. For O'Hara he bought an entire wardrobe of working
clothes, and a .45 in a holster. He bought them each a pair
of razors, a strop, a hone and a mug, brush and shaving
soap.

Getting bathed, shaved and dressed in their new clothes
used up part of the afternoon. O'Hara fell asleep on the bed
while Hewitt was trimming his mustache. Hewitt studied
him carefully. O'Hara's complexion had already lost much
of its mottled look, his belly some of its bloat. The old
trooper was fighting the hardest fight of his life, and he
might fool everybody and win it. *He's just the man I need*

for this job, Hewitt decided. *If Durango Slim is a white slave recruiter, Peter will never give up on him either.* . . .

Marshal Ed Parry was at the hotel before daylight, riding one good horse and leading another for O'Hara. He had two big pack mules, one to carry their trail gear and one to bring back Joe Crandal's body.

With him was Chief of Police Zeno Fox. He and Hewitt sized each other up warily as they shook hands. Fox would never be nicknamed "Foxy," Hewitt felt sure. He was not a big man, but he was tough, even a little touchy.

Hewitt gave O'Hara five ten-dollar gold pieces to give to the Washo chief, Lord Cecil McTigue. He and Chief Fox watched the two men ride off without ceremony. They would eat breakfast on the far side of Sacramento, Parry said. *Where Peter can't get a drink,* he might have added, Hewitt thought.

"Ed says you're on a case you don't want everybody to know about," Fox said. "How can my department help?"

"Have breakfast with me," said Hewitt, "and let's talk about it."

Fox took him to the hotel dining room, where they could sit at an isolated corner table and watch the entire room. He gave Fox the story as completely as he could, including his conviction that Durango Slim was a white slave recruiter. When he mentioned the Acey-Deucey, he felt he was getting close to one of the subjects on which Fox was touchy.

"Yes," the chief said, "it's a whorehouse. I don't apologize. On the frontier—and this is still the frontier, Mr. Hewitt—men outnumber the women and this is the only way things can work out."

Hewitt took a chance and said, "But there's still something about the Acey-Deucey that you don't like."

"Several other places here, too. The last few years, we've been getting younger, prettier girls, and they make good money because this is a money-making town. But they don't stay! They keep changing. Where do they go from here, do you think?"

"To San Francisco and then on to Australia, Hong Kong, Singapore, Shanghai—all the ports of Asia."

"That's my hunch. I wish I understood how it's run."

"Like any export business, Chief. I've heard that a young, pretty girl, already trained in the trade, is worth up to ten thousand dollars in Australia and Asia."

"You always think of white slavers when a girl just disappears. How are they talked into the business?"

"Recruiting them is a special trade, Chief. Face the fact that a few go willingly, knowingly, into a life that exactly suits them. I've heard of them becoming millionaires in Asia. Cow towns, trail towns, railroad division points, mining and lumber camps are full of woman who wish they could go to Asia for a few years, get rich, and come back here to live," Hewitt said.

"Most of them never come back. They die young on the other side of the world, and other girls take their places. That's why they want young ones for export. They bring more money and they last longer.

"I have traced two missing girls into the trade myself. One came from a good Chicago family, one from a German homestead family in Kansas. I brought them both back home. So far as I know, they both made good wives and mothers later. They were both recruited by the same man."

"Ever catch up with him?"

"Yes, again in Kansas. We were both 'courting' the same girl. Somehow he got the idea that I was trying to recruit her, too. He offered me a thousand dollars to leave town. She would have been worth twenty-five hundred to three thousand if he could have broken her into the trade and got her to San Francisco."

"What happened to her?"

"Why, she became one of the most successful female detectives I ever worked with. I've worked other cases with her since then."

"What happened to him?"

"I took the thousand dollars, don't you see, but I never left town. He tried to abuse the girl, and she pulled a thirty-two and killed him. Not as sad a case you might think, Chief. Her own cousin had been seduced and recruited by the same man."

Chief Fox was silent a long time. Then he said, "Place over the Acey-Deucey is run by a pretty Irishwoman, only name she's got so far as I know is 'Pretty Bridget.' Runs a quiet, orderly place, too expensive for the average trade, and never makes me any trouble. But it worries me because the girls come and go, come and go."

"Does a stranger have any trouble getting into Pretty Bridget's place?"

"Not if he behaves himself. No roughnecks, you understand. If you want to meet her, let's just wait right where we are. Pretty Bridget keeps a good team and carriage, and it's her habit to take a couple of her girls—different ones every day—for a ride after they close up early in the morning. Then she always comes in here for breakfast. That's her table yonder."

"Then let's wait."

They drank coffee and talked about the white slave

traffic for another hour. No one had to tell Hewitt when Pretty Bridget arrived. The carriage stopped with a jingle of harness at the side door. A waiter hurried to open it.

"Now go on back and get your beauty sleep, darlin's," a throaty contralto voice said in a lilting Irish brogue. "Pete, cool me team down and brush them good before ye put 'em in the stable. An' then ye'd best black the harness. It's lookin' neglected of late."

"Yes, ma'am," came the coachman's reply.

The woman who swept into the room was no longer young, but she was still extremely attractive. Dark, curly hair with a dramatic streak of gray over the left ear. Full figure, but the slim waist of an active woman who was careful what she ate. Stylishly dressed, and carrying a furled parasol in one hand and an expensive, plumed hat in the other.

A rosy face grown a little chubby since Hewitt had last seen her, but there was no mistake about who she was, and now suddenly he had two problems on his hands instead of one.

"What do you think of her?" Chief Fox asked, quietly.

Hewitt replied with a question of his own. "Know what a limerick is, Chief?"

"Sure. Pretty Bridget collects them. Why, do you know her?"

"Yes. She's not Irish at all. She's mostly German and she learned that brogue from her husband. Chief, that's Peter O'Hara's runaway wife."

CHAPTER VIII

When Fox merely stared at him, trying to figure out what this meant, Hewitt said, "No mistake. I know her—used to, anyway. If Peter doesn't drink himself to death in a week, he'll kill her."

"No, he won't," Fox said. "I'll jail him the minute he shows up."

"No, Chief, we're after a double murderer—remember? I need him." Fox was shaking his head angrily but Hewitt went on, "And I need her help to crack the white slave circuit. I need yours, too."

"Is that part of your job, Hewitt?"

"It is now. That's the way I'm going to get at Durango Slim. Bring the whole mess down on his head and let him try to explain it to whoever is running it."

"And who is that?"

"I don't know. Peter says she ran off with a one-eyed man. They left from Reno. Bob Stanley was his name, an unemployed railroad surveyor."

"Bob Stanley sounds like the kind of name you get when you jail somebody, and his buddy has already signed in as John Smith. Only one-eyed man I know is A. B. Creed— and man, he's a millionaire lumberman! He's building his own sawmill up in Calaveras County."

"Friend of yours?"

Fox's face did not change. "No. Ask Archie Chancellor about him."

Hewitt watched the woman covertly as he talked. She did not look thirty, yet he knew she was ten years older than that. He was sick with pity as he thought of what it would do to O'Hara to see her like this.

"Bother you if I go over and say 'hello' to the lady, Chief?" he asked.

"It won't bother me."

Hewitt signaled a waiter and asked him for a sheet of paper and a pencil. He did not write easily, something about which his partner often complained, but anger served him instead of inspiration. He showed what he had written to the chief and then got up and crossed to "Pretty Bridget's" table.

A waiter was just pouring coffee for her. She gave Hewitt a cold look that nevertheless had something too coy in it. A girl half her age could have got away with it, and it told him all he wanted to know about her intelligence. She was stupid as well as vain, and O'Hara was well rid of her.

"I understand you collect limericks," he said. "I've got a dandy for you, Rozeen."

The name he had called her seemed to go over her head until she had read the paper:

> *A darlin' young colleen named Schmidt*
> *Never knew when to quit.*
> *   She kept pushing her luck*
> *   Until she was stuck*
> *Up to her navel in trouble.*

Oh yes indeed, stupid she was! "Is something wrong, Pretty Bridget?" the waiter asked, as he saw her slide down in her chair, turn ashen and begin gasping for breath. Any woman who could not think faster than this had no business running a whorehouse.

"She's fine. I'll take care of her," Hewitt said. "If I can't, Chief Fox can. On your way!"

The waiter scuttled away. Hewitt pulled a chair out and sat down, not across from her but close beside her.

"Let's talk business, Rozeen," he said.

"Who—who are you?" she managed to ask, in a tremulous whisper.

"Remember when they tried to frame Major Foos, the week you and Peter got married? He had to testify at the court-martial before he could get leave to go on your honeymoon—you remember that, I'm sure. I'm the detective who cleared Major Foos and convicted Captain Pettinger and that horse broker from Omaha."

"Oh, my God, my God!"

"I don't think God can help you as much as I can, Rozeen. Peter works for me. He left Sacramento this morning, but he'll be back in a week. He'll kill you if he sees you. You know that, don't you."

"Chief Fox will protect me," she said through chattering teeth. "He'll see that Peter leaves me alone."

"Rozeen, a regiment of infantry couldn't keep Peter from killing you if he sees you running a sporting house. Maybe I can. I'll be up to your place to see you in about an hour. You be thinking it over."

"No, I—I've been up all night. I've got to sleep. My place is locked until four."

"Unlock it in an hour," he said, rising.

"No! We—we can't talk there."

"We *will* talk there. Rozeen, I'm trying to save your life. Either you help me do it, or you have less than a week to hide yourself as far as a train can take you. Don't talk to anybody until I have talked it over with you. Not Jack Purefoy—not A. B. Creed—not anybody."

When he reached the door, Chief Fox was waiting for him. He had paid their breakfast bill and was putting away a thick slab of currency, tens and twenties and even a few fifties.

"Go ahead, ask me where I got all this money," he said, as they walked down the street together.

"I heard you were a rich man, Chief. I heard you were an honest one, too," Hewitt said.

"I'll tell you anyway. I bought Walkashaw Remedy Company stock four years ago, at a dollar a share. It's worth forty a share now and it pays me a dollar a share dividend every quarter."

"Interesting," Hewitt said, indifferently.

"Archie Chancellor's family in San Francisco are big stockholders, too. I'm going to have Archie sell mine as quietly as he can. Know who the majority stockholder is, Mr. Hewitt? A. B. Creed."

"You make up your mind in a hurry, Chief."

"The name is Zeno. Hewitt, I'm an old bachelor, but a friend of mine had a young niece that he had adopted stolen by the white slavers. It killed his wife. He has wrecked more sporting houses, from Wichita to Oakland, than the police. Not a hell of a lot I can do to A. B. Creed, but maybe you can. If I can help, it's a debt I owe to the oldest friend I've got."

"That would be Sam Berry, I take it."

"You do get around, don't you?" was all Fox said.

They walked on. Nearing the Sacramento Specie Bank, Fox stopped. "Give me ten minutes," he said, "and then you go on in and talk to Archie. I'll go out the other door. I don't mind that he knows we're cooking up trouble, but I don't want it talked around town."

Hewitt turned into a tobacco store and bought a box of cigars. He made himself agreeable to the owner, making sure he would be remembered favorably, for ten minutes. A man in Hewitt's business could not have too many friends.

When he arrived at the bank, Chancellor was on his feet, heading toward a closed door at the rear of the building. He jerked his head for Hewitt to follow him. It was the board room, furnished with a big redwood table and nice chairs.

"What do you know about Walkashaw stock?" he asked Hewitt, the moment the door closed.

"Not much. What do you know?" Hewitt countered.

"Started by a fellow named Butler, Pearl Butler, ten years ago. He made the stuff and sold it himself on the road. Moved it from Kansas City to San Francisco about five years ago, raised two hundred thousand dollars, and then sold control to a syndicate. Everybody who got in on the original stock issue got rich."

"Did you ever meet Butler?"

"No. He was into something else by then, and he had a manager run the business for him.

"Know anybody who did meet him?"

Chancellor frowned. "Why, I have an aged uncle in San Francisco who used to know him in Kansas City."

"Can you wire him and ask if Butler was a one-eyed man?"

"No, but I can wire my cousin. Uncle Will's getting cranky and stubborn." Chancellor hit the desk with his first. "You figure it's A. B. Creed?"

There were times when you had to improvise, fabricate, invent. You had to look and sound sure of yourself, overbearing. Even a smart man like Chancellor had to be impressed now and then. Hewitt barked.

"Mr. Chancellor, I'm trying to move into a white slave ring that has been making somebody fifty thousand dollars a year for a long time. There's a one-eyed man in it somewhere. It occurs to me that a traveling salesman for, say, Walkashaw's Remedy would have all the excuse he needed to ride the trains. Do you know of any connection between Creed and this woman they call Pretty Bridget?"

"He owns the building she's in. I won't say he's a partner in the place, but he *has* to know what's going on there and it's a high-rent business, Mr. Hewitt. I know that the Acey-Deucey, downstairs, has had its rent raised twice since Pretty Bridget came in."

"I understand Creed has a lot of influence around here."

"Not in this bank, he doesn't."

"Well, I won't ask why."

Suddenly Chancellor grinned. "Mr. Hewitt, we're bonded by your company. If you demanded to know why I turned down A. B. Creed's business, I would have to have an answer for you or face cancellation of our bond, wouldn't I? All right, here's my answer—I just don't like the son of a bitch."

Hewitt could not help laughing. "My partner might not understand that answer, but I do."

"He came in here first when he was raising money for his sawmill. He could get credit anywhere else in California, but I turned him down, because I just don't like his slippery ways or his snotty way of talking to me. And if that endangers my surety bond, go ahead and cancel."

"On the contrary, glad I won't damage a client if I have to spraddle all over Creed."

"You're going after him as a white slaver?"

"I'm going after somebody," said Hewitt, "and if it turns out to be him, I'll nail his hide to the barn. How much Walkashaw stock does he own?"

"I didn't know he owned any."

So Zeno Fox kept a few things to himself! "My information," Hewitt said, "is that he's the biggest single stockholder. My firm has some clients who have bought Walkashaw pretty heavily. I'm going to wire my partner today to start easing them out."

"Do it quietly. Don't break the market," Chancellor said. "I'll get my family to start moving theirs. Job it out in small lots, through brokers who don't ask too many questions and who can come up with the cash. But before we unload all of ours, the price is going all to hell. We're in pretty deeply."

"Will your connection with this become known?"

"That I advised selling? I can see that it's known. What do you think would happen then?"

"I think we'll smoke A. B. Creed out. If he's borrowing money for his sawmill, he had to put something up as security. I wonder if it was Walkashaw stock, and I wonder what his bankers are going to do when the price starts falling."

Again Chancellor laughed. "Mr. Hewitt, we think alike. Let's walk down and get those wires off."

They went to the station together, and Hewitt was not surprised to see Chief Fox there, chatting with the telegrapher. He nodded coolly to them and left. When Hewitt paid for his telegram to Conrad, he slipped the telegrapher a ten-dollar gold piece.

"I know your files are confidential," he said, "but I would like to feel that this wire is extra-confidential. Wonder if you couldn't hold it out of your duplicate files for a week or two?"

"Sir, nobody sees my letterpress files except my inspectors, when they come around."

"But if somebody really wanted to break in here at night, it would be pretty easy, wouldn't it?"

"That's what the chief said," the telegrapher replied, worriedly. "All right, I won't even hide them in the station. They'll have to beat it out of me to see them."

"That could happen, too. Can't you make a mistake on your series numbers, so these don't show as missing? Just in case you are burglarized."

The telegrapher agreed. "You, I suppose, make it a habit to anticipate things like that," Chancellor said, as they left. "It wouldn't have occurred to me. I've got it get back to work. Anything more I can do for you?"

"Couple of questions, sir. Where is A. B. Creed now, and do you know anything about a fellow by the name of Cleve Huks? He's also called Durango Slim."

"Creed is up at his timber claim. I never heard of the other fellow." Chancellor paused on the sidewalk before turning back to his bank. "Probably no one else in Sacramento would agree with me on this, Mr. Hewitt, but I think I ought to warn you about something."

"What's that?"

"If you expose yourself behind this Walkashaw matter, if Creed gets the idea you're after him—"

"That is the purpose of it, Mr. Chancellor."

"Then he'll go after you any way he can, and I have said all along that he employs the worst cutthroat men of anybody in the cutthroat lumber business. I don't think he's too good to have you shot in the back."

Hewitt said soberly, "It's one of the back-shooters I'm

after. You heard the story about the man who tied the rat
out in his yard. His neighbor told him his cat couldn't resist
it. 'I know that,' the fellow replied, 'and there's a damn
noisy dog that barks all night and chases cats. He'll be here,
too, and he's the one I'm after.'"

The banker squinted at him. "I take it you can handle a
gun. Most men in your business can. Very few of them that
I have met can also understand high finance, and how to
shoot down a man by raiding the stock he has pledged for a
loan."

"I don't understand high finance," Hewitt said, "but I do
know how to find men who do. I'll appreciate any news you
get along this line."

They parted with a friendly nod, and Hewitt headed toward the Acey-Deucey. He had eaten a big breakfast not
long before and already was hungry again. The long ordeal
had honed him down to too fine an edge, and his appetite
warned him that he was not yet the man he had been
when he started out on Durango Slim's trail.

He turned a corner and had the Acey-Deucey in sight.
He came to a stop and instinctively slid back around the
corner, watching a man who was just tying his horse in
front of the saloon. The first thing he noticed was that it
was a good-looking, nimble little buckskin with a big brand
that he could not see clearly from where he stood. Probably
some cattleman's cutting horse until the last few days, and
as unlike Deputy Marshal Joe Crandal's horse as possible.

The man tying him badly needed a shave, and no doubt
a bath and some food and rest and all new clothes. He was,
in short, in the same shape that Hewitt had been in when he
got here. His striped suit was a wreck. His belt was pulled
up to the last hole. His shirt collar was filthy.

But it was Cleve Huks, Durango Slim, and it was a little

spooky to see the man whose picture he had drawn from O'Hara's instructions materialize so suddenly. His first thought was of Marshal Parry and Peter O'Hara. They had surely not been long on the road when Durango Slim came down out of the foothills.

Had they met? If not, why not? One thing was sure— Durango Slim's Winchester '73 was not lashed to the buckskin's side.

There stood the man who had beaten little Virginia Baldwin to death. There stood the man who had corrupted Emma Baldwin and left her dead of shame and despair. There stood the man that Simon C. Rankin was paying him handsomely to bring to the gallows.

Durango Slim hitched up his pants, took time to twist and light a cigarette, and then pushed through the double, swinging doors of the Acey-Deucey.

"Hey there, Slim!" came a joyous cry from inside. "You took your time getting here, old partner!"

Hewitt could not hear Durango Slim's reply. He got control of his anger, stepped out from the protection of the corner and walked swiftly down the street on the sidewalk across from the Acey-Deucey. He could see nothing inside, and was fairly sure that if Durango Slim was watching him he would not know him in his new clothing.

He crossed the next intersection and then waited while a big dray wagon loaded with cargo from the river docks could conceal him as he turned left. When he was opposite the side door of the saloon—the one leading to Pretty Bridget's upstairs establishment—he crossed the street quickly and tried the handsome brass knob. The door was locked.

CHAPTER IX

He rapped sharply on the door. Nothing happened. He knocked again. When still no one answered, he picked up a rock the size of his fist from the street, and pounded smartly on one of the varnished door panels.

He waited a moment and then pounded again. He was sure someone was standing just inside the door, hoping he would go away. Probably one of the maids, perhaps Pretty Bridget's personal maid, ordered to keep him out but given no instructions on how to do it.

He put his face close to the door. "Anybody inside there had better get out of the way," he said, clearly. "I'm going to shoot this lock out in a minute."

He heard a tremulous, feminine voice say, "He says he's going to shoot the lock out!" He did not hear the reply, but the door opened. A big, rawboned woman in the plain black dress of a housemaid barred his way.

"You cain't come in," she said. "Miss Bridget, she said to tell you we done closed for the day. Go 'way and don't bother folks, why don't you?"

Some poor, simple countrywoman to whom this job was the best she had ever had, her wages the most she had ever dreamed of making. Hewitt swept off his hat.

"Now, you know I'm coming in, ma'am," he said, "and the lady upstairs knows it, too. Are you going to force me to get rough? I assure you, she'll be sorry afterward if you do."

"Oh, for Christ's sake, let him come up, Marilla," came Pretty Bridget's voice.

Marilla stepped inside. Hewitt came in. "Better lock up behind me," he said. "I don't think she's going to want to be interrupted."

He heard the lock click behind him. The narrow stairs had been deeply and richly carpeted and the walls covered with flowered silk paper. He ran up them lightly, two at a time, and stepped into the main parlor of a house that would have done credit to sporting circles in San Francisco or New York. It was not large, but through a door he could see down a short hall to another parlor about the same size.

Rozeen Schmidt O'Hara, who had become "Pretty Bridget" since alighting in Sacramento, was sitting on a mahogany settee luxuriously upholstered in rich purple plush. The crimson curtains of the room had been drawn shut, and two ceiling lamps, with hand-painted globes and green lace shades, had been lighted.

Rozeen was sobbing distractedly. Trying to comfort her were two of her "girls," both young, both haggard from lack of sleep, both close to tears themselves. Hewitt did not despise whores by any means, but neither did he subscribe to the sentimentality that found hearts of gold in all of them. Many of them might have been unfairly recruited by white slavers, but most of them were whores because that was what they were best fitted to be and what they wanted to be.

"Let's step outside, girls," he said. "I want to talk to the madam in private."

They glared at him resentfully. Rozeen stopped sobbing long enough to wave them away. The door had no sooner closed behind them than she shot to her feet. "Let's go somewhere else to talk," she said, brokenly. "Anybody can blunder in here."

"Mr. Creed, for instance," Hewitt suggested.

She did not answer, but she cried harder as she led the way down a back hall and used a key to unlock a plain door that could have led to a storeroom. Inside the large room behind it, however, was only one piece of furniture— a big craps table made of varnished redwood, its top and the six-inch wall around it lined with green felt. On it lay a familiar box, still sealed, holding, Hewitt knew, twelve pair of dice.

He closed the door behind him and went straight to the single window in the room, to orient himself. Getting into a room like this was usually much easier than getting out of it. He drew the heavy curtains aside and looked out. This room overlooked the back alley, acres of stacked lumber and, in the near background, the river. The window sash was heavy. He would have appreciated a heavy chair with which to smash it, if a quick escape became necessary, but he thought he could make do kicking it out.

"What's your name, did you say?" the woman asked, making an effort to get control of myself and the situation in which she found herself.

"I didn't say," he replied, "but I'm Jefferson Hewitt, of Bankers Bonding and Indemnity Company. Creed can probably tell you about us, but I can tell you a lot more about him. He'll be broke in a month, Rozeen."

"Listen here," she said, "I don't know what Zeno Fox told you, but he's a grafter and a liar. He is too busy stuffing his pockets with—"

"Don't bother," Hewitt cut in. "I want to talk to you about Cleve Huks. What do you know about him?"

"Huks?" she said, wonderingly. "Nothing. Who is he?"

He believed her. "How about Durango Slim, and do you know about him?"

"I don't know him and I don't want to, from what I hear about him. What have I got to do with him?"

"He's downstairs right now in the Acey-Deucey. He's going partners with Jack Purefoy."

She said, energetically, "Oh no, that backstabbing sneak doesn't stop in *this* town! That fool of a Jack, if he thinks he's going to let murdering riffraff like Durango Slim hang around downstairs—"

"You mean A. B. Creed won't stand for it."

"All right, God damn it, he won't," she flared. "Durango Slim beats up on girls. Once he cut his initials in a girl's bare back. You can't have someone like that hanging around a respectable place like this. You can't even allow him in town!"

He let her run out of breath. "Now, listen to me carefully, and keep quiet until I'm through, Rozeen," he said. "Durango Slim *is* here, and A. B. Creed, or Bob Stanley, is on the skids and going down so fast, there's nothing he can do about it. Peter O'Hara will be back in Sacramento any day. How long do you think you can hide from him? And what do you think Creed is going to do when he finds out that he's broke?"

"Broke? Him? That's the craziest thing I ever heard. Why, he's one of the richest men between San Francisco and Reno."

"He was when he left here the other day, maybe. He'll come riding hell-for-leather any day now, when the word gets to him that the banks have shut off his credit. Do you know anything about Walkashaw Remedy?"

"I only wish I owned a few shares of it. *He* owns forty per cent of it! He told me so himself."

"The company's broke, Rozeen."

"I don't believe you."

"By tomorrow evening, half a million dollars' worth of shares will be on the market with no buyers. This is my business. Who is your banker here? Ask him what he knows about Bankers Bonding and Indemnity Company."

"I don't fool around with bankers. Believe me, I keep my money where I can lay hands on it any time."

He remained silent. He knew she was terrified of a confrontation with Peter O'Hara. All she needed was time to think it over, and she would realize that if A. B. Creed was broke, she was through in Sacramento, too. That still left playful Mr. Durango Slim, who might, after all, end up as a full partner downstairs.

He went to the window and leaned against the wall, holding the curtain aside to watch the busy scene between here and the riverbank. He could tell by the woman's breathing that she was about to succumb to terror again, and he almost felt sorry for her. Poor, vain, stupid woman, her dream of wealth and luxury had become a nightmare in the wink of an eye, with herself in the middle of a triangle of three dangerous men.

"Listen, Mr. Hewitt," she said, tremulously, "can you do me a favor?"

"Depends on what it is."

"Can you find out when that boat leaves for Stockton, and can you get me aboard it when it goes? There are two staterooms. I don't care what it costs, get me one of them. Fix it with the skipper so I can slip aboard after dark, so no one sees me, please? Please? Please?"

"That's no good," he said. "How long do you think it would take any of them—Creed or Durango Slim or Peter —to find you in Stockton or San Francisco?"

"But, Jesus, I've got to get out of here, I can't stay here, I'm as good as dead—"

"I can get you out," he said, "but first, let's have a little talk."

"What about?"

"A. B. Creed, or Bob Stanley, or Pearl Butler—"

"How did you find out about Pearl Butler?"

He grinned at her. "Pearl Butler founded Walkashaw Remedy, you know. I told you it was broke, didn't I? Rozeen, just how close are you to this man?"

"He—he's crazy about me. He really, really is, Mr. Hewitt. For the first time in his life, he's in love. He says so himself, and—"

"I believe you. That's why you're afraid to stay and face him if he's headed down the flume, isn't it?" She nodded and he continued, "Go on, tell me more."

When the words came, they came in a rush. She had known Creed/Stanley/Butler for a year and a half now, and the man must have gone mad over her to talk as freely as he had to her. She had first been flattered by his devotion when he was posing, in Reno, as an unemployed railroad surveyor with big money to spend. He had been kind, soft-spoken, gallant, and attractive despite the black eye patch.

In fact, the eye patch made him singularly magnetic. He had lost the eye, he said, fighting with British troops in India. He had a story to cover everything. Not until this moment had Rozeen realized that no man could possibly have been all the places and done all the things her lover claimed to have been and done in less than a hundred years.

Once she calmed down, Rozeen had an extremely practical mind, made all the sharper by fear. The plan Hewitt laid out for her would require considerable help from Zeno Fox, and perhaps considerable luck, too. It was worth all the work and trouble because he had a hunch that A. B. Creed was just as madly in love with Rozeen as she said he was. When he found himself broke, and deserted by Rozeen, he would be right where Hewitt wanted him.

Hewitt liked Rozeen better when she demanded to take her girls along to safety with her. Disloyal though she might have been to O'Hara, she still had compassion for the women who worked for her.

"Can't be done," he said, "and they wouldn't want to go, either. If you put up the money, I'll book them into a stateroom on the boat and hire a man to stand guard over them until they disembark. San Francisco is where they'll want to go, anyway. You know that!"

"I reckon you're right," she sighed. "It's where I wanted to go, once. That's where the money is. But I reckon it's not for me—not now, anyway."

"Speaking of money, how will you take yours along? No sense in leaving here broke."

"I won't leave here broke. I've got a valise full of it, and you've got to get it out safely with me, Mr. Hewitt."

He agreed. He made her promise to keep the doors to both stairways locked, and to impress on her girls that they opened them at the risk of their lives. They had food and a kitchen, and they would just have to stand the boredom until he could get them to the river boat.

The same stolid maid went ahead of him to unlock the street door, but before they reached it, they heard someone pounding on the door that opened on the stairway to the interior of the Acey-Deucey. The terrified girls heard it, too, and fled like a covey of flushed quail to the other side of the fortress that Pretty Bridget's place had suddenly become.

"Open up, Bridget. Come on, Bridget, I know you're awake," a man was shouting. "Got a friend I want you to meet."

"Jack Purefoy?" Hewitt asked, softly. The maid nodded. "All right," he whispered, "you just unlock the door and step aside. I'll open it."

They walked softly down the hall to the other door. Hewitt motioned the woman to step beyond the door and give him room. At his nod, she slipped the thumb latch on the heavy brass lock. The click resounded loudly through the silence of the hall.

Outside, there was silence too. Then:

"Bridget?" came a man's voice. "I want to talk to Bridget a minute. Tell her it's Jack."

Hewitt shook his head at the maid, who remained silent. In a moment, he saw the ornate doorknob turn slowly. He heard the small gasp of surprise as the door opened.

He reached out and jerked the door wide, so swiftly that Jack Purefoy lost his grip on the knob. Purefoy was about Hewitt's own age—say, his early forties—and he had probably once been a tough man to handle. Too many years of good living, of making good money behind a bar, had added to many soft pounds to his weight.

Behind him stood the man whose picture Hewitt had drawn by mountain firelight, his hand guided by Peter O'Hara's memories. The same narrow, arrogant, tiger's eyes, the same sallow skin stretched taut over a big-boned face, the same adenoidy, half-open mouth full of strong, prominent teeth.

No chance now to get at Durango Slim, who stood behind Purefoy. Hewitt had learned long before that there were times that self-control was impossible, and that the only thing to do was make the explosion count. One thing, you did not waste time and energy on words. Whenever you took time to call a man a name, you were handing him a gift of seconds that could be the difference between life and death.

He made as if to swing a looping, overhand right at Purefoy. The startled barkeeper yelled and spun away from it, and straight into the short left jab that Hewitt drove into his guts. Purefoy doubled over and clawed out with both hands, trying to get hold of Hewitt to hang on. Hewitt drove a hard right into his nose and then caught him by the collar with his left hand.

He swung the stunned and breathless Purefoy into Durango Slim and pushed. He heard Durango Slim yell as he lost his footing. Both men went tumbling down the carpeted stairs and Hewitt went after them, shouting to the maid to shut and lock the door behind him.

Purefoy stopped rolling halfway down. He lay there on his back, head down, and by the look on his face he was completely unconscious. Durango Slim managed to arrest his fall and struggle dizzily to his feet. His hand went into the pocket of his coat and came out with a Colt .44 revolver.

Hewitt, from three steps higher, brought his booted right foot up and rammed it forward. The heel caught Durango Slim on the nose and mouth. The .44 went off, sounding like a cannon in the echoing stairway, the slug ripping at a slant into the stairway wall, high overhead.

As Durango Slim fell backward, Hewitt went after him. They were almost to the bottom of the steps before Hewitt could reach his face again with his boot heel, this time on the right cheekbone. He saw the .44 slide free as Durango

Slim became unconscious. He picked up the gun and tossed it up the stairs, all the way to the landing beside the door.

For a moment, all was silence. Then Jack Purefoy rolled over on his stomach with a moan, caught himself as he began to slide headfirst down the carpeted steps, and tried to struggle to a sitting position. His face and eyes were blank as he tried to figure out what had happened and where he was and who Hewitt was.

Hewitt yanked Durango Slim to his feet and dragged him the rest of the way down the steps. Beside the door to the saloon, he propped him up against the wall and began slapping his face. The man's nose was still streaming blood, and the whole right side of his face would be black and blue tomorrow.

But he was at least partly conscious. He could see and hear, and perhaps remember. Hewitt stopped slapping him and rapped him sharply in the stomach with his knuckles. Durango Slim doubled over again, choking for breath, but Hewitt jerked him back up and held him against the wall.

"Get this, Huks," Hewitt said, "and make damn sure you never forget it. I'm going to let you go now, but then I'm going to run you down and take you back to Colorado to stand trial for the murder of Virginia Baldwin. You'll be found guilty, and you'll hang, and I'm going to be right there to watch you strangle."

Durango Slim was stronger than he looked, and tougher. He wrenched free of Hewitt's grip and reached for his boot top. Hewitt brought his knee up into Slim's crotch and caught him on the jaw with his elbow as Slim again doubled up. He threw the man down and pulled off his boot and took the long, thin-bladed knife out of it.

He opened the saloon door and threw the boot through it. Again he caught Durango Slim by the collar and hauled him to his feet. He gave him a running start through the door and saw him fall on his face on the saloon floor. He closed the door and turned, sliding his .45 out of its holster to face Jack Purefoy.

"Up on your feet, Purefoy," he said, "and let's see both hands in sight as you come down the steps."

The saloonkeeper stood up warily. "What the *hell* is this? Who are you? Hey, what's this all about?" he said.

Hewitt motioned him on down the steps, keeping the .45 aimed at Purefoy's chest. "Your old buddy," he said, when Purefoy reached the bottom of the stairs, "is wanted for two murders—a fifteen-year-old girl in Colorado and a deputy United States marshal in California. I haven't got anything against you . . . yet. My advice is to cut loose from him—give him the bum's rush—don't even be seen talking to him. Roust him out of here right now, before he gets you into trouble with him."

Purefoy shuddered. "Oh hell, nobody gives Durango Slim the bum's rush, mister. He—why, he's the worst— why, I'd no more talk back to him than I would a rattle-snake."

"You saw him take a beating just now," Hewitt said. "He's a hell of a girl-fighter but he doesn't do so well against a grown man, does he? Outside, Purefoy—and get rid of him. And don't show your face on these stairs again until you're sent for."

He prodded the reluctant Purefoy through the door and closed it. There were two heavy drawbolts to lock it. He pushed both home and went up the stairs to recover Durango Slim's .44 and make plans with Pretty Bridget, also known as Rozeen O'Hara.

CHAPTER X

Chief Zeno Fox had many misgivings, but once he agreed to Hewitt's plan he had some suggestions for improving it. He had two detectives on his force. One was trying to identify a murdered man whose body had been found in an alley near the river front less than two blocks away from the Acey-Deucey. The other was assigned to keep an eye on Durango Slim.

The murder victim was taken to a funeral parlor nearby, to be embalmed and laid out for public inspection. He was a middle-aged man wearing what had been a good suit not long since, but he had gone badly to seed. Another drunk who had hit bottom on the river front, the doctor thought. Still, someone might know him.

The captain of the *Amanda Stark* agreed to assign a stateroom to Pretty Bridget's six girls, and to post guards twenty-four hours a day until he started downriver when the last of the lumber was stacked on deck. A smaller cabin, close to the captain's own, was assigned to Pretty Bridget and would be kept locked until she appeared.

Late in the afternoon, a portly woman wearing a denim jacket and skirt and heavy shoes went puffing up the steps from the sidewalk to Pretty Bridget's place. In a few minutes she came down, muttering angrily. "I'm a decent woman," she was heard to say, "and nobody can say otherwise even if I do make my living scrubbing floors. You didn't tell me what kind of place this was."

The detective who was investigating the murder case asked her to come to the funeral parlor, to see if she might possibly know the dead man. She grumbled, but she went.

Evening came. Pretty Bridget, wearing a maroon taffeta dress and a flowered hat with a heavy veil, led her girls down the stairs to where her own carriage was waiting. They got in and were driven to the gangplank of the *Amanda Stark*. They filed aboard and went into their two cabins. The doors were locked, and the captain posted a burly guard before each.

Shortly after nightfall the eastbound train stopped in Sacramento before beginning the long climb over the Sierra Nevada where mile after mile of plank snowsheds kept the rails open through the worst storms. A plain pine coffin holding the remains of the murdered man was put aboard the baggage car, consigned to Omaha. The train started.

Jefferson Hewitt was admitted to the baggage car the moment the train was in motion. He handed the baggage man the other fifty dollars that he had been promised, and the two of them took screwdrivers and quickly opened the shipping box and then the pine coffin inside it.

Pretty Bridget, also known as Rozeen O'Hara, got out. She was still dazed with fright, but she recovered quickly when Hewitt showed her the eight suitcases and one heavy little trunk that had been smuggled aboard. In the trunk was a little more than $60,000 in gold coin and currency that she had amassed in Sacramento. Hewitt gave her a ticket for a Pullman compartment and escorted her to it the moment the aisles were clear and most of the passengers had gone to the dining car.

"I guess I should thank you, Mr. Hewitt," she said, as

they shook hands, "but damned if I don't wonder if you haven't pulled a skin game on me. You and that chief of police—what a slippery pair of bastards you are!"

"If you feel that way, Rozeen," Hewitt said, "all you have to do is take the next train back to Sacramento and try to persuade Creed and O'Hara that you're on the level with both of them."

She burst into tears. "Oh, God, how did I ever get myself into this?" she wailed. "That damned, drunken O'Hara—he's to blame."

"He wasn't a drunk when you got married. You got yourself into it when you drove him to the liquor."

She said distractedly, "I'm a woman of refinement, Mr. Hewitt. Why should I be married to a common sergeant? All my life I'd had bad luck. To think that being married to a sergeant could look good to me! He's a boor, Mr. Hewitt, an ignorant man, crude and—"

"Never mind, Rozeen, you're free of him now, and he's free of you. You'll land on your feet somewhere."

Hewitt tipped his hat to her and went to the vestibule where the conductor was waiting. "About two more miles, sir," the conductor murmured. Hewitt slipped him a wad of folded currency. When the time came, the conductor pulled the brake cord and the train jolted to an emergency stop. Hewitt swung off. The conductor leaned out and signaled with his lantern and the bewildered engineer started up again.

Hewitt stood beside the tracks until the train had vanished. A rider appeared, leading a saddled horse. "You're right on time to the second," Hewitt said, as he swung up into the saddle of the led horse.

"You don't know Chief Fox," the other man replied.

"Damned if this hasn't been a day! Never thought there'd be so much excitement when I joined the force."

"How did it go at the *Amanda Stark?*"

"Like shooting fish in a barrel," the other replied, cheerfully. "I changed into my own clothes and left Pretty Bridget's in a neat stack on the bed in the cabin. Soon as the chief came aboard, I slipped out and went ashore with him. There's going to be one mighty mixed-up river captain, when he finally opens that door and finds he's short one distinguished female passenger."

"What about the dead body?"

"Oh, hell, he's buried by now. I don't know his name, but the chief does. Some bum that has been hanging around Sacramento for several weeks. Won a little wad in a blackjack game last night and got killed for it, probably."

"What about Durango Slim?"

"Last I heard, Jack Purefoy got him a room at Ch'ang Hong's place. That's a real dump, Mr. Hewitt. Jack brought him a slab of beefsteak for his eye and a quart of rotgut. The chief took charge of his horse, to investigate if it was stolen."

"He'll find that it wasn't, I'm sure."

"Yes, but it'll take him several days, and that fellow ain't going nowhere in the meantime." Again the young policeman laughed. "More to bein' a cop than a fella might think —right, Mr. Hewitt?"

"Right!"

"Chief says you're the most famous detective in the West, sir."

"Your chief does me too much honor."

"I doubt that. He says by God, you have your own way of doin' things, but he means to go along with you and learn a few tricks himself. I mean to keep my own eyes open. If I'm going to make law enforcement my career, I can't learn too much, can I—right, Mr. Hewitt?"

Back in Sacramento, Hewitt went straight to his hotel room and slept the sleep of the just. He was awakened in the morning by the hoarse hooting of the whistle of the *Amanda Stark* as it eased away from the wharf, its decks piled high with stacks of Ponderosa pine and sugar pine lumber. Hewitt got to the window in time to see Pretty Bridget's six girls rush from their cabin to watch as Sacramento slid past them.

They were in high spirits, eager to get to San Francisco and the big money of which they had all dreamed. There was nothing anyone could do for the poor, deluded creatures. Maybe one of the six would find life better there than it had been before. The other five would be easy victims of the white slave recruiters who knew their work so well. Six months from now they would be in Australia, Shanghai or Hong Kong, looking back on life in Sacramento as a luxurious dream.

There was no crowd in the Acey-Deucey that night, and Chief Fox sent several men—not policemen—in to buy a drink or two and try to talk to Jack Purefoy. They reported that he was despondent and that he appeared to be frightened to death, too. In any case, he left the bar in charge of a bartender before ten o'clock and went out as if on a sudden impulse.

The plainclothesman watching Ch'ang Hong's flophouse saw Purefoy go almost to the door and then stand there trying to nerve himself to go in and face Durango Slim. He could not do it. No one followed him to see where he went, but one thing was sure—he did not go into Ch'ang Hong's place and he did not return to the Acey-Deucey.

After breakfast, Hewitt went to the railroad station to see

if any telegrams had arrived for him. Again there were two.
The first, from his partner, Conrad Meuse, said:

> PUZZLED BY STOCK SALES WIRE STOP TAKING ADVICE
> BUT PRICE FIRM HERE STOP ALSO WIRED CHICAGO DO
> SAME STOP HOPE YOU NOT MISLED ADVISE SOONEST

And from Simon C. Rankin a heartbroken and almost
incoherent wail of grief and fury:

> DOCTOR SAYS MUST REMAIN BED INDEFINITELY OR
> FACE CONSEQUENCES STOP JUST AS SOON DIE BUT
> WANT BUSINESS OVER FIRST STOP FINISH IT THERE
> STOP YOU OWE THIS TO EMMA AND HER BABY

To Si Rankin, the dead Virginia would always be a baby.
How long "always" would be was the question. If Si had
consented to be put to bed, it meant at least a heart attack.
He must be in bad shape indeed. And now Hewitt was
relieved of the need to take Cleve Huks, *alias* Durango
Slim, back to Colorado for trial, conviction and hanging.
Now all that Si wanted was to know he was dead before his
own heart quit on him.

When Hewitt got to the Sacramento Specie Bank, Archie
Chancellor was in conference and could not be disturbed.
Hewitt had to wait nearly thirty minutes before the meeting
broke up and Chancellor emerged. He was red-faced and
angry, and his eyes glittered as he motioned for Hewitt to
come into the board room, where the air was heavy with
cigar smoke.

"This is showdown time for me, Mr. Hewitt," he said, the
moment he had closed the door. "Hell is popping in San
Francisco. If we're wrong on Walkashaw, I'll have every
damned bank in California gunning for me—and if enough
of them gang up on you, they can smash you."

"And if we're right?" Hewitt asked, quietly.

Chancellor smashed his fist into his palm. "I gave them fair warning! Listen, there are five banks holding Creed's paper on this sawmill deal, two of them here and three in San Francisco. The two here are catching hell from the ones in San Francisco, and I've been catching hell from them. I just let them out the alley door, that's how serious it is—the presidents of the two biggest banks in Sacramento slipping down the alley!"

"I take it," said Hewitt, "that there has been some action on Walkashaw Remedy stock."

Chancellor sat down heavily. "My family bought in at a dollar a share, mostly. Some of it cost 'em two dollars. We unloaded most of it yesterday at forty-three dollars, but it started to slip, and we got only thirty-eight for the last couple of blocks. I've been getting wires all morning since daylight. They're three hours ahead of us in the East, you know, and the slide has started back there. Look at what has happened to the price just in the last three hours!"

The street market in San Francisco must have been a madhouse by daylight. The first wire said BID TWENTY-ONE ASKED THIRTY-EIGHT. Bidding had declined rapidly, dragging the asking price down with it. The last quotation, filed less than an hour ago, said BID FIVE ASKED FOURTEEN. That meant that the few speculators willing to take a flier in Walkashaw stock would now pay only five dollars a share for it. Those still holding it were asking only fourteen —and not getting it.

"We do business with a brokerage house in Chicago," Hewitt told the banker. "We started dumping there, too. I don't imagine it remained a secret very long."

"My God, Mr. Hewitt, do you realize what we have done? Here's a man who, I'm told, was worth five or six

million dollars day before yesterday. Today he's broke, and
he owes a little more than a million for a sawmill that he
now can't finish building. All because we destroyed the
value of the company stock he had pledged for security on
his sawmill loan."

Hewitt took out two cigars and offered one to Chancellor. He held a match for both. "We didn't destroy anything, Mr. Chancellor," he said. "We merely exposed the
truth, that's all."

"And, as Pilate said on another occasion, 'What is
truth?'"

"The truth is that Walkashaw probably never did make
enough money to justify that price. The truth is that Creed,
or Bob Stanley, or Pearl Butler, or whatever other name he
uses, has made his money in the whorehouse business. I
think he has pumped enough of that money into Walkashaw to make it look like a hell of a business, because he
needs a legitimate storefront for his white slave deals. If
they want that kind of business," Hewitt said, "let them
have it. But if we're bonding them, let them look for another bondsman, too."

Chancellor grinned a tight little grin. "Well, you can't
win if you don't bet. Like I told you, I never did trust that
slippery son of a bitch."

"What happens now?" When Chancellor shrugged, Hewitt went on, "Are they sending word up to him at the sawmill site? That ought to bring him down a-hellin'."

"They didn't say. I doubt it. I think they would just as
soon he stayed up in the big timber, out of their way, until
the dust settles. Maybe San Francisco will have other ideas,
but they would have to go through the banks here to get a
messenger up to him, I think."

"How hard would it be to find him?"

"Why, are you thinking of—?"

"No, but Durango Slim might. He's running out of places to hide."

Chancellor was silent a moment. "Watch yourself, Mr. Hewitt," he said, at last. "Zeno Fox told me all about this fellow, Durango Slim. It occurs to me that if he wants to pick up an easy thousand or two, why, Creed carries that much around in pocket money."

"That has been tried before, too," Hewitt said.

Before he left the bank, the stationmaster delivered another telegram to Chancellor from San Francisco. It was unsigned, and it merely said, NO MARKET. That meant that there were no more bidders for Walkashaw Remedy Company stock, and those who still owned it were stuck with it.

"Then we just wait," said Chancellor.

"And so does Creed, and so does Durango Slim," said Hewitt. "If it's any comfort to you, waiting is a lot more painful to them than it is to me."

Again Chancellor grinned. "Me too—I *think*," he said.

Hewitt waited, knowing the man had more to say, and that he was going to enjoy saying it. "By the way," Chancellor went on, "my cousin wires that Uncle Will said that Pearl Butler was a one-eyed man. I don't mind saying, Mr. Hewitt, that I feel a lot better since I learned that."

CHAPTER XI

Marshal Ed Parry and Peter O'Hara returned with the body of Joe Crandal a day and a half earlier than Hewitt would have believed possible. Zeno Fox sent word to him, and Hewitt hurried down to the funeral parlor where they had taken the body. Both men were haggard with fatigue, but O'Hara looked fit all the same. There was a different look in his eyes, a swagger of self-confidence to his big body.

He took a rifle from the pack on the horse and tossed it to Hewitt. "There now," he said, "an' what do ye think of that? Bit of a surprise, eh?"

It was a Winchester Model '73 that badly needed cleaning. "Durango Slim's?" he asked.

"Yis."

"How'd you get it?"

"Me friends, the Washos, got it away from him. They seen him kill the deputy here, too. Lord Cecil McTigue himself seen it, wid one of his boys and another feller."

Hewitt looked at the hard-faced Parry, who nodded grimly. "They'll be here when they're needed to testify," Parry said, "and they'll be believed. Your case will have to wait, Mr. Hewitt. He'll hang for this one, right here."

"How did they get the rifle?"

"Dropped on him from a tree," O'Hara said, "afther the

others herded him that way. Ask Ed. He talks their lingo better than I do."

The Washo people were peaceful, good-natured and extremely reticent. How strange to think that they had spent the night by the fire on top of the Sierra divide with Hewitt and O'Hara and had not said a word about witnessing the murder! Yet that, Parry said, was the way they were. Not until the rifle had to be explained did they bother to carry tales of the white man's actions to other white men.

They had seen Durango Slim punishing his horse to get over the summit. They had seen him leave the trail when the horse played out, tie his horse and dismount with his rifle. Had they been armed with a gun of equal range and force, they would have taken him then. As it was, they could only watch.

They saw Deputy Marshal Joe Crandal ride into the trap, walking his horse, sparing it for the long ride still ahead. Lord Cecil had shouted to him, "No, no, no—go back, go back!" He saw Crandal haul his horse down and stand up in his stirrups to listen.

"No, no—go back!" Lord Cecil shouted again.

But even as he called, he saw Durango Slim scuttle through the brush with the Winchester in his hand. Saw him drop to his knee and take a longer shot than the Indian believed possible. Saw Crandal pitch from the saddle with a lethal hole in his abdomen.

Saw Durango Slim leave cover in the brush and race across the slippery patches of frozen snow toward the fallen man. Crandal hoisted himself to his elbow and lifted the gun from his holster, but he never got to fire it. Durango Slim brought the Winchester up from no more than ten feet away and shot him through the heart.

The Indians saw and heard Hewitt when he drove

Durango Slim back down the mountain with his shouts and the shots from his Remington .30-30. They did not know him and it was none of their business what the white men did, was it? Lord Cecil sent one of his men after Durango Slim, to keep track of where he was going. And O'Hara had been right—Durango Slim headed blindly into a box canyon and spent a miserable night huddled in the shelter of a tree trunk, squatting on his heels and holding his horse's reins in his cold hands.

The main body of Indians spent that night around the fire with O'Hara and Hewitt. They still did not want to get involved in the white man's problems; so they kept their peace. But the next day they saw Durango Slim on the trail, riding the dead deputy's horse and pushing it hard. He was not much of a tracker, but he could follow the tracks that O'Hara and Hewitt and their pack horse had left.

O'Hara was their friend. Durango Slim was cold and hungry and desperate. They still were not looking for trouble, but they decided they could even the odds against their friend a little bit, anyway. They drove Durango Slim crazy, calling to each other from the brush on both sides of the trail. They let him get a look at one or two of them—just a glimpse as they faded deeper into the brush that covered the steep canyon wall here.

Just as they had planned, Durango Slim went after them. Lord Cecil McTigue's own son and another youth fell on him from a tree, disarmed him and let him escape. It was the Washos' way of handling something that could have been a problem to one of their friends. When O'Hara returned with Marshal Parry, they handed over the big Winchester and submitted to questioning.

"He met a couple of cowboys headed over the divide," Parry said, "and swapped horses with one of them. The Indians saw that, too, but we'll play hell ever catching up with those fellows who have Joe's horse. They couldn't help but know they were dealing for a stolen horse, and they'll make themselves mighty skeerce in Nevada."

"You better get some rest, Ed," said Chief Fox, "and let me gather this son of a bitch in."

"You know where he is? He's in Sacramento?" the marshal cried. "Oh, no! He's my prisoner, and I'll be there to arrest him. Where is he?"

They argued. It seemed to Hewitt that Parry was close to collapse with exhaustion, and he tried to persuade him to see things Fox's way, too. Fox saw that it was hopeless.

"You know Ch'ang Hong's place?" he asked.

Parry did. "That boar's nest? Maybe we'll clean that place out for you today, Zeno," he said.

"Ch'ang ain't the worst in town. I like to know where to lay hands on people. Let's do this the quiet way, Ed. Swarm in front and back at the same time, no shooting if we can get out of it," Fox said.

"There'll be shooting," Parry said. "Ain't no way to avoid it with this fellow."

"I've whipped him once," Hewitt interjected. "Let me go in first. He won't go for a gun with me. He's got to prove he can handle me with—"

"You stay to hell away from there," Parry ordered. "Zeno and I will take this fellow in." He raised his tired voice slightly, seeing the expression on Hewitt's face. "If you show up there, Mr. Hewitt, you're going to be arrested for interfering with a federal officer in the performance of his duties."

"Mr. Parry, you're ready to collapse. You're good and mad, and I don't blame you. But your judgment isn't the best right now, and you know it," Hewitt said.

Parry acted as though he had not heard, and Zeno Fox shook his head as though to say, *Don't waste your breath, he's got his mind made up.* . . . Hewitt and O'Hara took the horses and started toward the public stable where Parry had rented them.

O'Hara was in a buoyant mood. He did not look like a young man by any means, but the punishing climb up to the divide and back had proved that he was not an old one, either. They turned the horses in, and then O'Hara wanted to go to a restaurant he knew for something to eat.

"A thick ham steak," he said, "an' about four eggs, sunny side up, wid fried 'taties. It don't seem like supper widout the 'taties—and this time, Jeff, I won't throw 'em up."

A fine brown horse, almost a buckskin, was tied outside the restaurant door. They stopped to admire it. "Jack Purefoy's," O'Hara said. "What wud he be doin' in here? He's too good for the likes of this place since the Acey-Deucey's doin' so well."

Something that was not quite a hunch slowed Hewitt's feet. He looked the horse over carefully, trying to decide why he felt unwilling to go into this place. "Four years old, almost five by now," O'Hara was saying, "and he'll never quit on you. The only horse I ever knew his equal was the black one Major Foos rode—remember?"

"I remember," Hewitt said. "Peter, how well do you know this Jack Purefoy?"

"Not well, but long," said O'Hara. "He used to have a bit of a store at Post Seven. You remember Post Seven, Jeff, north of Fort Sumner? In New Mexico, 'twas."

Hewitt remembered. Purefoy might then have known O'Hara's wife when she was still Rozeen Schmidt. If so, it was a dangerous bit of information to possess.

"Let's try somewhere else, Peter. We're entitled to the best today," Hewitt suggested.

"This is the best. Don't let the outside fool ye, Jeff. They feed a man well here, they do."

O'Hara opened the door and went in, and there was nothing Hewitt could do but follow him. It was a small place with an L-shaped counter with a dozen stools. Behind it, tending his stove, was a plump man with a fringe of reddish hair around his bald and freckled head. His blue eyes, when he turned to look at them, had a twinkle in them.

"No drunken old sojers wanted here, O'Hara. Be off wid yez or I call the cops," he said, in an Irish brogue richer than O'Hara's.

"Oh, go to hell, Flaherty," O'Hara said, genially. He looked at the one customer who was dozing drunkenly with both elbows on the counter and his face in his hands. "Why, 'tis a reunion, like!" he went on. "What is it you're weepin' over, Jack? Let me see, man!"

Too late, Jack Purefoy tried to hide the two big photographs that were on the counter. Hewitt got only a glimpse of them as he pushed between O'Hara and Purefoy. Both were of Rozeen Schmidt O'Hara, also known as Pretty Bridget.

Both were studio portraits of the naked upper half of her body that flaunted her magnificent bosom. In one she wore the mantilla of a Mexican girl and held a rose by its stem between her teeth. In the other she had on a coquettish little riding hat with a half veil.

"Come on, O'Hara, hands off my pictures," Purefoy said, trying to cover them with his hands. "They're not your business, they're mine. You don't even know her."

Why, Hewitt thought, the empty-headed woman had

Purefoy as crazy as ever O'Hara or Creed had been. He wondered how many other men had copies of these photographs and believed, as Purefoy undoubtedly believed, that they had been taken only for him. Purefoy was in a drunken stupor, his eyes swollen with tears, so much liquor in him that he could think only of the woman he had known lately as Pretty Bridget. The woman who was just one flight of stairs up from his Acey-Deucey saloon.

O'Hara's elbow shoved Hewitt aside. His big right hand swung out in a backhand slap that caught Jack Purefoy across the mouth and knocked him off the stool. O'Hara snatched up the two pictures and stared at them, his eyes full of madness.

"Why, they're me wife, they're Rozeen!" he bellowed. "Where'd you get 'em, Jack? Where'd you get the pictures of my wife?"

Hewitt tried to come between them. "Not now, Peter," he said, sharply. "It's not his fault. I'll tell you about it later."

O'Hara, clutching the pictures in his right hand, swung a left hook that caught Hewitt under the ear and turned the world black for him. As he fell and as the shadows fell around him, he saw O'Hara pick Purefoy up as he would a child, and slam him against the counter. The Irishman, tired as he was, had enormous strength made greater by his rage and horror.

"I'll choke ye to death, man, if ye don't tell me the truth," he shouted. "Where'd you get the pitchers of me wife, God damn you?"

He closed his big hands around Purefoy's throat. "Listen to me, Peter, listen to me," Purefoy begged. "I'll tell you the truth if you'll only let go of me."

Some of the drunkenness had gone from his voice.

O'Hara let go of his throat and took him by both shoulders to shake him.

"Out wid it! Where is she? The truth, Jack, if ye expect to live the day out."

Across the counter, Flaherty swung a short eighteen inches of pitchfork handle, no doubt weighted with an ounce or two of shot. He caught O'Hara on the top of his head, dazing him enough to make him release Purefoy.

"He's tryin' to tell yez, Peter," said Flaherty. "'Tis not his fault if 'tis not what ye want to hear."

Purefoy scuttled to the other end of the room. "The hell with you, O'Hara," he said. "She's a whore and a whore madam and she's been runnin' a house above my own saloon these long months. Only today she's in San Francisco somewhere, her and her girls, gone down the river on the *Amanda Stark*. Ask Hewitt there! He put her aboard himself."

Hewitt got to his knees, seeing the despair that came over O'Hara's face as he looked once again at the photographs before crushing them in his hand. "Ye lie, ye lie to the bottom of yer black heart!" he screamed. "Go fer yer gun or I'll kill yez in cold blood, ye son of a bitch!"

To Hewitt it seemed that they drew at the same time—O'Hara the .45 that Hewitt had given him, Purefoy a little double-barreled pistol that he drew from under his coat. Only O'Hara's gun went off. The room boomed and echoed with the roar, and then boomed and echoed again.

Jack Purefoy crumpled into a pile on the floor with blood already gushing from his mouth and nose, and with two .45 slugs in his chest. O'Hara holstered his gun and looked at Flaherty.

"He lied, didn't he, Timmie?" he begged. "'Tis all a

black lie he told, ain't it? These ain't me wife," he entreated, waving the pictures. " 'Tis somewan that looks like her, no more than that, an' he lied to me."

A man came swiftly and calmly through the back door as O'Hara leaned across the counter with the two crumpled pictures in his hand. He wore new Levi's and boots and a new, rakish brown hat with a wide brim and a creased crown. Under the hat his cold blue eyes glittered, and his pouting lips were parted in a bruised and bullying smile.

Durango Slim! And Hewitt had marked him painfully, deeply.

Hewitt clawed in his pocket for his sap and went after him. Durango Slim jumped him and knocked him back to the floor, pumping both fists into Hewitt's belly. O'Hara dropped the pictures on the counter and turned, still half-dazed with shock, and reached for his .45 again.

"Here, now, what do ye think ye're doin' to me friend?" he said.

Durango Slim took a knife from his sleeve and drove it between O'Hara's ribs again and again. Hewitt knew when O'Hara fell. He knew when Durango Slim calmly turned his back on O'Hara. He knew when Durango Slim found the wallet in the breast pocket of Hewitt's own new coat.

The killer took time to remove O'Hara's gun belt, holster and gun, but not to put them on. Carrying them in his hand, he ran lightly to the front door. He turned there, tossing the gun in his hand to get a better grip on it, and aimed it carelessly at Tim Flaherty behind the counter.

"Keep your hands in sight, and stay out of it," he said. "It's between me and him, there."

Hewitt rolled away from the counter and got the .45 out of his holster. He knew he came close enough to bring out the coward in Durango Slim when Slim's shot went into the ceiling. Durango Slim ran out into the street and Hewitt heard the hoofbeats of Jack Purefoy's prized horse, hard-ridden.

Hewitt crawled on hands and knees to O'Hara's side. The big Irishman was already dead, his heart cut to ribbons by a man who enjoyed the act of killing. The pictures of O'Hara's wife had fallen to the floor beside him.

"It's just as well he died," said Flaherty from behind the counter. "Ye know why, I'm sure."

"I know," Hewitt said.

"Good God," said Zeno Fox, "it looked like they'd been butchering a hog in there, Mr. Hewitt."

"I know. I was there," Hewitt said, irritably. He pushed the doctor aside and tried not to show his impatience. "I'm all right, Doctor. I've taken worse beatings."

"You don't know which way he went?" Zeno asked.

"No idea. Surely someone saw him."

"That's the hell of it, Mr. Hewitt—no one did. But I'm sure someone would have if he had gone *down* the river toward the steamboat landing."

"Then he's heading back toward the Sierra."

"Only thing possible. Ed Parry will swear in some special deputies and be on his way in an hour."

"He's in no shape for a hard ride, and a posse never goes any faster than the slowest horse. Chief, where can I find a horse as good as the one Durango Slim is riding, and a guide who knows the Sierra and how to track a man through it?"

"There's no horse as good as Purefoy's," said Fox, "but there's no better guide than yours truly. I'll get the horses ready as soon as you're fit to go."

"I'm fit to go now. But you're a chief of police here, Zeno. Your writ doesn't run outside of Sacramento."

Fox patted the .45 that hung in his flank from a heavy belt that twinkled with new brass cartridges.

"This does," he said.

CHAPTER XII

Within five minutes it was clear that there would be a second posse taking the trail. Bumbling, fumbling, loud-mouthed Sheriff Ernie Goodin came raging into the doctor's office to which they had taken Hewitt. Until now, Hewitt had managed to avoid meeting him.

"I want to know what's going on here," Goodin roared. "I've heard about you, Mr. Hewitt, and I don't appreciate it a damn bit, you coming in here behind my back and making trouble."

Hewitt found it hard to keep either his legs or his temper steady. "I haven't trespassed on your jurisdiction, Sheriff," he said. "I haven't done a thing to account to you for. Sorry, but I'm in too much of a hurry to argue with you."

The sheriff, a hulking, deep-chested man with a double chin that needed shaving and a tangle of uncut hair, got between Hewitt and the door. Hewitt had met a lot of local peace officers, some good and some bad. He was used to making quick judgments of them, and Goodin did not strike him as an evil man.

But he was an ignorant man, jealous of his power and position and not very bright. He would be a far more impressive man in a political campaign than he would in a crisis, once he was elected.

"You ain't got a thing to do as important as answering a few questions," the sheriff trumpeted. "You get this damn drunken Irish trooper stabbed to death by somebody that *you* know and nobody else does—*nobody*." He had to shift his cud of chewing tobacco to go on: "Why'd he kill Jack Purefoy? Answer me that, Hewitt! He was working for you, they tell me. Jack was a friend of mine and a respectable businessman. Why did O'Hara murder him?"

"He didn't murder him. Purefoy brought it on himself, but I haven't got time to argue with you now."

Zeno Fox tried to intercede. "Come on, Ernie, there's a time and a place for everything. Mr. Hewitt's just took a bad beating and—"

Goodin cut in. "Oh yes, I know what you're up to. You been lookin' for a chance to run against me for a long time, and I knowed it all along. Well, let's see what the voters think of bringin' in a Pinkerton and gettin' Jack Purefoy murdered right in your own town. That's what I want to know—why? That's what I want this feller to tell me— why? Why did O'Hara kill him and who is this feller that killed O'Hara?"

Hewitt shook his head at Fox. "I'll tell you why, Sheriff," he said. "Your friend, Purefoy, was taking liberties with the name and reputation of O'Hara's wife."

"Wife? Wife?"

"Yes, wife."

"He didn't have no wife, the drunken bum!"

"Yes, he did, and you knew her. Not as Mrs. O'Hara, though. She was Pretty Bridget to you and she paid you fifty dollars every Friday night. Pretty Bridget's place was an important stop on the white slave circuit, and Jack Purefoy knew it and so did you. It's the filthiest trade in the world, Sheriff, and maybe the voters aren't going to like it when your part in it comes out."

The sheriff lunged at him. Hewitt stepped back and reached for the sap in his hip pocket. He feinted at the sheriff's face and, at the last minute, snapped his wrist to bring it down—hard—on the side of the neck.

Goodin moaned with pain and went to his knees. He was perfectly conscious, but he was paralyzed by pain. Hewitt put his hands on his shoulders and pushed, and the sheriff toppled over on the floor.

Hewitt stood over him with his coat unbuttoned, his hand on his .45. "And I'll tell you something else, Mr. Goodin," he went on. "Mr. Creed's going to get some other bad news in the next day or two. He's not going to like anything that has happened while he has been up in the Sierra. Think about that a little—see where it leaves you. Creed is through in California, do you understand?"

In a moment, Sheriff Goodin was able to move without shrieking with pain. It was Hewitt himself who helped him to his feet. All the fight was gone out of the big man. His face had the expression of a slapped baby.

"Zeno," he said, "what's goin' on here? What's this feller sayin' about Pretty Bridget? Where'd she go, anyway? Seems to me you're the one going to have to answer to Mr. Creed for that, not me."

Fox let Hewitt answer. "You'll never find her and neither will Creed. Take my word for it, you're mixed up in the rottenest business in the world, and I have her statement, with her signature, put away where you'll never find it. Tell Creed that when you see him!"

"Who is this feller that killed O'Hara?"

Hewitt did not mind telling the poor, bewildered man a few things. "True name is Cleve Huks, also known as Durango Slim. Wanted in Colorado for the murder of a fifteen-year-old girl he was trying to recruit for Creed's white slave operation. Wanted in California for the murder of a deputy United States marshal. Now also wanted for the cold-blooded, premeditated, unprovoked murder of Peter O'Hara. Tell Creed that, too!"

"Got to find enough able-bodied men to bring in this feller," Goodin said. "Swear me in a posse. Run him down before he loses us in the Sierra."

He shambled out. Hewitt looked at Fox, who shrugged. Hewitt's head was clearing and the clash with the sheriff had helped clear it. Before he did anything else, he wanted to talk to Archie Chancellor. Zeno Fox walked with him to the bank.

"Don't worry about Ernie Goodin," Fox said. "He'll go straight to A. B. Creed's sawmill, that's all."

"So will Durango Slim," said Hewitt.

"You really think he was in cahoots with Creed?"

"If he isn't now—well, I'm sure that he has been in the past, and he will be as soon as he can get to Creed. I want you to join Chancellor and me in a quick conference. In my job, there are times when you can't find the handle on a case to save your life. When that happens, you push. You put your shoulder against whoever is handiest, and dig your heels in and push. If that doesn't work, you push somewhere else.

"I've pushed hard on Creed. At first it was just a way to spring Durango Slim out of hiding, but now I'm after something bigger. I don't want to lose sight of Durango Slim. But when I put the chains on him, I want to drop the roof on some other people, too."

"The white slave ring."

"Yes."

"Jeff, you'll never abolish whores. There'll always be women that don't want any other life and there'll always be a need for them wherever there are jobs where a man can't bring a wife and raise a family."

"I know that, Zeno, but it's not prostitution I'm trying to abolish. It's *slavery,* women who have lost their right to decide where and how they want to be whores. And it's men like Creed and Durango Slim—yes, and women like Rozeen O'Hara!—who victimize them. There will always be victors and victims, too, I suppose. But a man can hack away and bloody a nose here and there."

"I reckon even a poor whore has her rights. You never think of it in that way, do you?"

"I know that I'll never forget it from now on," Hewitt replied.

Chancellor saw them come into the bank and got up and went straight to the door of the board room. He held it open for them and then closed it behind them.

"You look like hell, Mr. Hewitt," he said, "but I'm sure you have a right to. I just heard about O'Hara. He was a friend of yours, wasn't he?"

"Yes."

"Well, what can I say?"

"You can tell Chief Fox what is happening about Creed, or Stanley, or Butler, or whatever his name is. I've been giving him the background so far."

"I'm through as a banker if the chief talks in the wrong places," Chancellor said.

"He won't even talk in the right places."

Chancellor's nerve was being strained to the utmost, that was clear. "I'm catching hell, Mr. Hewitt. I've had a couple of threats from banks big enough to break me, and that's just what they promise to do if I don't ease up. Creed is into them for a million and a half, near as I can make out. Christ, I didn't realize it, but he's building the biggest saw-mill on the West Coast and going to run his own narrow-gauge railroad to bring logs to it! No more ox teams, except to get the logs to the steam cars, no more ten-horse teams hauling green lumber out over mountain roads. Biggest thing this industry has ever seen!"

"Good business, is it?"

"Why, hell yes!"

"Took a man of vision to put it over, too, wouldn't you say?"

"That's the thing that gets me. How a man who could conceive a plan like this could be involved in the things you tell me Creed has been involved in—"

"Mr. Chancellor, it took vision to conceive a trans-continental organization to make women earn their own way to the Pacific ports, where they could be shipped like cattle to the Orient. It took vision to take Walkashaw's Remedy and build it from a peddler's wagon to a national product made and sold by one of the most profitable corporations in the country."

Chancellor looked unsure of himself. "What's your point, Mr. Hewitt?"

"My point is that Creed can have the vision, but he can't run an honest business. Unless this sawmill and logging operation are taken away from him, more people are going to lose money than they would in a dozen Walkashaw gyps."

"But the Walkashaw stock *did* make money. It—"

"Oh, sure, for you who got in at a dollar a share. But what do you know about the remedy? What'll you bet that it turns out to be sassafras extract, tincture of opium, alcohol and flavoring? Your family came out fine on it, but all these years they've been receiving dividends on a gyp pain-killer that doesn't cure anything. Is that the way you want to make your money?"

"No, of course not, but—"

"Get hold of a bottle of the damn stuff and have it analyzed. I told you, too, that I'll bet some of the profits from the white slave business went into the Walkashaw company to keep the price of the stock up. Does your family want that kind of money, too?"

"Go on."

"You like this sawmill plan, do you?"

"I told you, it's the greatest thing that—"

"Then go after it!" Hewitt cut in, sharply. "Somebody's going to pick up the pieces there—why not you? There'll be a bloody fight for ownership there, but if you don't know how to fight that kind of fight, after Creed is out, you have no business being a banker."

"I won't be one, if—"

"Which banks are giving you the most trouble over it? Come on, man, this is no time to be discreet! I have to know, just as you have to fight."

"Delano and Cahill's State Bank of San Francisco and the Eagle National Bank of San Francisco."

"I never heard of either one of them."

"They're not old banks, Mr. Hewitt, but they've got a lot of capital behind them."

"If they're new banks, it's better than an even-money bet that Bankers Bonding and Indemnity Company wrote the surety bonds for their officers. If we didn't, my partner has ways of passing tips to our competitors, in return for a few they have passed to us over the years. If I write a telegram, can you get it down to the office and on its way immediately? Zeno and I have other things to do."

The wire to Conrad Meuse said:

URGENTEST CONFIDENTIAL DELANO AND CAHILL AND
EAGLE NATIONAL BOTH OF SF DANGEROUSLY INVOLVED
SAWMILL FINANCING STOP CRASH OF EITHER OR BOTH
COULD BE DISASTER STOP MOST NECESSARY BOTH BE
ADVISED BOND ENDANGERED UNLESS THEY WORK OUT
OTHER ARRANGEMENT SAWMILL STOP DON'T ARGUE OR
SOMEBODY HOLDING VERY BIG BAG VERY SOON

"Jesus, that's laying on the whip, Mr. Hewitt," Chancellor said, wiping his sweaty forehead with his sleeve as he passed the wire on to Chief Fox to read.

"Yes. If I were running either of those banks, and I got a wire threatening to cancel my bond over the sawmill deal, do you know what I would be wondering?" said Hewitt. "I would be wondering what the hell it is that Archie Chancellor, of Sacramento, knows that I don't know. Doesn't that give you any ideas?"

"One or two," Chancellor said, with a sudden smile. "Let's get this on its way. Have you any other suggestions, Mr. Hewitt?"

"Yes. Wear a gun and stay out of Creed's way."

"I'm not a gunman. I'd be more likely to shoot myself."

Before Hewitt could answer, Fox tossed the telegram back to Chancellor and said, "Then hire somebody who can use one to stay with you twenty-four hours a day. Hire two men, so they can spell each other off! It'll cost you. Kind of man you need is worth ten or fifteen dollars a day, Archie."

"Where am I going to find them?"

"You're not. I am. All you're going to do is pay them."

Chancellor broke into a broad grin. "Gentlemen," he said, "I think we're all going to get along very well indeed as partners in the sawmill."

A herd of at least five hundred yearlings and brood cows, moving up to the early grass in the lower Sierra meadows, filled the canyon ahead of them. There was no going around them.

"Maybe we can go through them, though," Hewitt said.

"Not likely. Those critters are spooky and fresh to the trail. Ever try to handle a herd in these damn canyons? But we can try," said Fox.

There were six men in charge of the herd. The one who was obviously the foreman was no more than a kid, a tough and wiry and hard-eyed youth who probably enjoyed trouble. He saw them coming up the grade behind him and turned his horse to ride down to meet them.

"Keep your goddamn distance," he said in a high, shrill, angry voice. "Next son of a bitch to scatter this bunch of crazy cow bastards is a dead man."

"We're not going to scatter your herd," said Fox.

"You never spoke truer words, stranger."

"Why, has someone already tried it?"

"Yes, and if I catch up with him—"

"Didn't happen to notice the brand on his horse, did you?"

"Say, what is this, anyway?"

Fox opened his jacket to show his badge, but not clearly enough for the kid to see that it was only a Sacramento city badge.

"We're tryin' to be friends with you, son," he said. "Why don't you be friends with us? Who was it rode through your herd and scattered it?"

"Little old humped-over crawdad of a feller with a straggly gray beard, riding a bay gelding with a Roofed Eight brand. You know what he did? He fired his gun, plumb emptied it, to clear the way for him. We been an hour and a half pullin' 'em together again," the kid screeched.

"Pay the man some money, Mr. Hewitt," Fox said. "Now, son, me and my friend are going to trail along behind you until you find a good place where we can ride through, and we're going to do it without making things no tougher on you than they already are."

The kid took the twenty-dollar gold piece from Hewitt suspiciously. "Is that feller wanted for some crime?"

"No, nothing like that. But there is a badly wanted man at large in these mountains somewhere, and you would be well advised to be on the lookout for him. If you see him, shoot on sight. And I mean that just the way it sounds, son. So you listen!"

Fox described Durango Slim, the kid scowling as he tried to picture the man. He whirled his sweaty horse and spurred it to catch up with his crew and his herd.

"The Roofed Eight brand is Creed's?" Hewitt asked.

"Yes. He raises beef for his logging crews, and a few hogs. Mostly he wants to breed race horses."

"The banks are sending a messenger up to him."

"I expect so. I know if I was in their shoes, I'd want a few answers from him about now."

"Let's see who finds him first—Durango Slim, or the messenger on the Roofed Eight horse."

Fox said, thoughtfully, "Either way, he's goin' to wet his pants. Here he is, right on top of the world, one of the richest men west of the Rockies if the cards keep on fallin' right. Why, he could get clear out of the white slave business and be a hundred per cent respectable! Only suddenly everything is shot to hell for him."

"We'll hope so, anyway."

"You know, Jeff, I'd never expect a range detective to know as much about banking as you do."

Fox wanted an explanation, and he was entitled to one. "We're first of all a bonding company, Zeno," Hewitt said. "I didn't know beans about it when we started, but my partner knew everything. He knew nothing about field investigations, and we had to teach each other. On my end of the job, you do what you have to do, learn what you have to learn, try to forget nothing, and bluff your way through when you come up short."

"How often does that happen?"

"Every now and then. Now, for instance."

"What are we short of now?"

"The Washos. Some of them were Peter's friends. We could use their help about now, but even if we had time, how do you find them to ask their help and tell them about Peter's death?"

"You don't," said Fox. "Long as I've lived here, I've never learned to understand how fast news travels in these mountains. The white man talks a lot, but the Washo does a lot more listening. He holds his tongue and bides his time, and very few people give him credit for knowin' as much as he really knows."

"But you do."

"Well," said Fox, "I try to, and the Washos still surprise me every now and then."

CHAPTER XIII

Chief Fox seemed to know every trail through the Sierra.

They rode through the herd on rested horses and climbed rapidly with the sun behind them. Fox had come to California as a boy of sixteen, he said, to hunt for gold. He had found silver instead, on the east slope of the Sierra Nevada, and had sold out too cheaply. Then he had brokered beef to the mining camps, buying wild Mexican cattle in the western valleys for fifteen dollars a head and driving them up the mountains to sell them for one hundred dollars.

He had lost cattle on the way, strayed, stolen, killed by bears or in stampedes on perilous trails through the high passes. But he had become a rich man—and he had learned these canyon trails as few men had learned them. He was not the methodical packer and tireless rider that Peter O'Hara had been, but he was at home here in a way that the Irishman had not been.

In the short time that Hewitt had been in Sacramento, the season of green leaves and bright flowers had already climbed to somewhat higher elevations. They camped in time to do their cooking before dark, Fox caring for the horses while Hewitt toasted bacon and made ashcakes. They had seen two spring fawns that afternoon, but Fox did not want to shoot them.

"There's more real meat on jack rabbit," he said, "and I don't care for any kind of milk-fed meat."

Hewitt had smiled to himself; Fox simply did not like to kill anything so young and made excuses, and Hewitt felt the same way. Wherefore they ate the rude fare of the trail and were both content.

And just as darkness fell, after the fire had gone out, they heard suddenly the rattle of unshod hoofs on a stony creekside trail. Fox grinned at Hewitt.

"What'd I tell you? They did that apurpose, to let us know they're comin'," he whispered.

Three Washos riding two horses stopped just out of range of a .45, indistinct silhouettes in the dark. The one in the lead took off his hat to scratch his head.

"Hi, Fox, you hear me?" he called.

"Sure, uncle, come on in. This is Mr. Hewitt with me," Fox replied, without getting off his haunches.

The two who were riding double on one horse dismounted first and held the other's horse while he came toward the dead campfire. It was the Indian that O'Hara called Lord Cecil McTigue. He did not bother with a greeting, but squatted down facing them across the ashes of the fire.

"Where you going'?" he asked.

"After the man who killed Peter O'Hara," said Chief Fox.

"I hear that, yes. Who kill him?"

"The man with the Winchester Seventy-three." The Washo did not answer. Fox went on, "Ed Parry is after him, too. He's headed back up toward Angels Camp."

Still the Washo did not comment, but it seemed to Hewitt that Parry's expedition was no news to him and that he did not take it very seriously. He wondered just how fluent the man was in English. Certainly he seemed to understand all he needed to understand, whether he could reply or not.

Fox went on talking, as though the only way to com-
municate with this man was to tell him all you knew or
thought you knew, and wait for him to correct you:

"It's our hunch, uncle, that the man we're chasing will
try to get to where Creed is building his sawmill. We don't
know if he knows how to get there or not. There's another
fellow headed there, too. One of Creed's men on a bay
Roofed Eight horse. Everybody's running around in circles
—you understand what I mean by that? Mr. Hewitt and I
want to catch this fellow before he finds Creed, if we can.
Catch him, now, not kill him! You like some bacon and
bread? It's cold, but there's some left over."

"Sure."

It was the first word the Washo had spoken since joining
them. He made a signal to the other two, who tied their
horses and came to the dead fire. Both were mere boys,
Hewitt saw, no more than thirteen or fourteen.

"I talk pretty good English," the older of the two boys
said, accepting a piece of ashcake and a chunk of bacon. "I
went to school a few years. You got the right idea, Chief of
Police Fox. That crazy goddamn murderer fool, he talk to
Pat and Harry this afternoon. You know Pat and Harry?"

Fox nodded. "Couple of hard-rock miners," he told Hewitt. "They could tell him how to find Creed."

"Yeah, they did. He got a good start on you. We better
go pretty early, you bet!" the kid said.

So the Washos would go with them! Hewitt was content
to rest while he could, and let the three Indians stand guard
over their camp. They were unarmed except for an ancient
Peabody .45 rifle clumsily rebuilt to use modern .45 center-
fire cartridges.

That night, Hewitt seemed to sleep away deep, sore spots
of fatigue that had been growing worse for weeks, even

months. They were not yet into the Sierra Nevada, but they had left the warm valley behind and were high in the foothills. He did not stir until he heard Lord Cecil McTigue saddling the horses.

Sunrise, when he sat up, was still an hour away. Zeno Fox was still deeply asleep. One of the Washo boys had started a campfire of dry wood. As Hewitt stumbled to his feet he heard the crack of a rifle that sounded familiar to him. He saw the young Indian and the old one exchange satisfied glances: *We eat fresh meat this morning!*

The other youth shortly returned to camp, carrying Hewitt's Remington .30-30 and a yearling buck deer. He held up one finger with a grave face, but with a knowing twinkle in his eye: One bullet, one deer! Yes sir, these Washos were going to be good trail companions.

Late in the afternoon of the next day they came to a ranch in the heart of what had been the gold country. There were still some working hard-rock mines on this slope, but they were far to the south of where the gigantic placer-mining pumps were gutting the rivers and destroying forever thousands of acres of groves and grassland.

They traded horses here. Hewitt and Fox had let the Washos guide them, pushing as fast as men and horses could go. The rancher who had bought up the old Mexican land grant here said that the messenger to A. B. Creed had swapped horses here only this morning. His Roofed 8 horse, gaunt and spent, was in the corral now.

He squatted to draw them a map showing the best way to reach Creed's sawmill site. "You're probably a fur piece ahead of the man you're chasin'," he said. "You've made a mighty smart ride of it from Sacramento. But you ain't going to have no carnival to welcome you to Creed's works. I do some business with him—beef and horses and the like—so I got to get along with him. But he sure is the most unsociable man I ever knowed."

"He'll probably get more unsociable very soon," Hewitt said.

They decided not to spend the night on the ranch, but to camp again in the mountains. No use embarrassing a man who had been more than helpful to them. Not long after they left the ranch, they intersected the road used by Creed to get, Fox said, to Angels Camp. They followed it until Lord Cecil McTigue's sharp ears heard someone coming down. They pulled off into the timber and dismounted to watch.

Soon a "bull team" of four oxen appeared, pulling a high-wheeled cart loaded with five huge saw logs. The wheels were eight or nine feet in diameter, Hewitt estimated. They would keep rolling long after smaller wheels had bogged down in soft earth or cramped in narrow ruts. The logs were delicately balanced, and chained to the cart with massive chains pulled taut by big iron jacks. A skid at each end of the cart prevented upending, but to Hewitt it was a marvel how such weight could keep equilibrium on just two wheels.

The smallest log was probably forty inches in diameter. They were all fine sugar pine or ponderosa pine, white, grainless wood that would saw into the most useful of all softwood lumber. The size of the fortune for which A. B. Creed was scrambling became clear when Chief Fox muttered, "Close to a million board feet of lumber on that load, and he's got standing timber enough to cut for a hundred years."

The cart went on down the slope. It would take it several days to reach the railroad, several more to the sawmill in

Sacramento that already had more Creed logs than it could handle. Build your sawmill closer to your standing timber, freight out lumber instead of logs on your own narrow-gauge railroad—ah, yes, a handsome empire indeed to have been built on the earnings of forlorn women and girls!

When the oxcart had passed, they took to the road again, but soon had to leave it for another load of logs. One of the young Washos rode on ahead then, to scout the road. In an hour he was back.

"More logs comin'," he said, "but they stopped to talk to that feller—you know, that's goin' up to see Creed."

"The messenger from the bank?" Hewitt asked Fox, who nodded. Hewitt looked at the Washo boy again. "How far ahead of us are they?"

"Twenty minutes, thirty. I don't know how long they're gonna stop and talk."

Well, that was logical enough. "How far now to Creed's sawmill?"

"It ain't a sawmill yet, but where he's gonna have it—well, about two hours, maybe three."

"What do you say, Zeno—let's catch up with the bearer of bad news and ride in with him?"

Fox nodded. "I'd like to be there, Jeff, when you talk to Creed."

"You have a right to be there. I want you to be there."

"Just to see that everything's legal."

"If it isn't," said Hewitt, "it will be Creed's fault, not mine."

They put their horses into an easy gallop despite the steepness of the incline. This country had already been cut over by lumbermen, and there were aisles of stumpage through which they could sometimes see far ahead. Just as they saw the next log cart, its driver put it in motion, whooping at the four oxen, prodding them with his long pole.

And beyond it they saw the little old man sent by the Sacramento banks to warn Creed that, like Samson, he was about to have his temple come down around his ears. They passed the bull cart with a nod at the suspicious driver and the two timber hands who were helping him. They seemed surprised to see anyone on the road, but they said nothing.

The messenger did not hear them until they were within two hundred yards of him, riding through a stand of white fir "trash trees" that had no market value and hence would never be cut. Briefly, not a stump was in sight, and the long afternoon shadows made it almost possible to believe that the rutted road was not there. The contrast between virgin timber and the spoil man had left behind him was vivid and moving.

The messenger was indeed old and small, but he was one of those tough little old men who had learned how to cope with life among tough big men. He turned his horse in the road and pulled a .45.

"Who the hell are you? What are you doing on this property?" he shouted. "Be off or I'll fire."

Hewitt slid the .30-30 from its boot and dropped to the ground, letting one of the Washo boys take the reins of his horse.

"Don't be a damn fool, man," he called. "I've got the range on you. Keep the gun in sight and pointed toward the ground until I get there."

He began walking toward the messenger, carrying the rifle at the ready. The old man whirled his horse suddenly and dug in his spurs. The horse grunted and made a startled, sprawling leap and began running.

Hewitt dropped to one knee and snapped a shot after

him. He knew he was a good shot, and a good shot could always count on a little luck. He heard the old man yell as the slug screamed past him. He hauled his horse down and turned it again, his .45 pointed down at the ground.

"Nobody bluffs me," he said, with no apparent rancor. "Just had to see if you meant business."

"We do." Hewitt levered another cartridge into the Remington's chamber and walked on. The old man tossed the .45 up and caught it by the muzzle so he could hand it butt first to Hewitt. "No hard feelings," Hewitt said. "We just want to ride with you to see Creed."

"Is that the goddamn chief of police in Sacramento with you? What the hell does he want with me?" the old man snarled.

"That's Chief Fox, and I told you, we only want to ride with you."

"He knows better than that. Creed ain't goin' to like this one damn bit!"

Hewitt held the man's gun until Fox and the Washos got there. Fox grunted a curt greeting, which the old man answered with a sullen nod.

"You've got a letter on you, too," Hewitt said. "We'll have that."

"You will like hell!"

"Now, you know better than that. Are you going to make us take it away from you? There's no disgrace in yielding at gunpoint."

The old man took the folded and crumpled envelope from his pocket and handed it over. Hewitt merely glanced at the wax seal and put it, unopened, in his own pocket. "Let's go," he said.

CHAPTER XIV

It was not just a sawmill growing here, it was a small city.
"But it will take time, a lot of manpower, and a lot of
money before it begins paying off," Hewitt said to Fox, as
they rode through the clearing toward the big, half-finished
office building.

"I heard it was going to be the biggest sawmill in the
world," Fox said.

The messenger stubbornly rode with them, but the three
Washos had remained back in the timber. Hewitt let the old
man lead the way toward the corral behind the log office.

Only the bunkhouse and kitchens, built last year, could
be called finished. The dam on the little river was almost
done and the big steam engine had been mounted on its
massive sills. An army of workmen swarmed over the site,
raising the log framework of the building that would house
the saws and other machinery.

Winter weather might stop logging, but if Creed got out
enough logs during the spring, summer and fall, he could
spend all winter sawing them and storing up lumber. If he
built his own railroad and covered it with snowsheds, he
could haul out millions of dollars' worth of lumber every
year. There were, Hewitt estimated, at least three hundred
men working here now.

One whose red plaid shirt and big, hulking frame made
him stand out came striding to meet them. He wore a

logger's high, calked boots and a red stocking cap, and he carried a thick roll of building plans under his arm.

"Hold up there," he called. "Who are these fellows, Cappy?"

"We can't hold up," the old messenger said, "because these fellers already held me up. I brung a letter for Mr. Creed, but they've got it."

The big man looked Hewitt and Fox over. "I know you, Mr. Fox," he said, "but I don't know this man. You know the rules about trespassers here."

Hewitt said, "I don't want to cause trouble for you, sir, but we're going to have to talk to Mr. Creed and I think he's going to want to see us. It will save everyone a great deal of bother if you tell him that his bankers are calling his loans and I represent the company that bonds them, Bankers Bonding and Indemnity Company, of Cheyenne. He'll know the name."

A gun in his face might not have stopped Creed's foreman, but that did. "Wait a minute," he said. "Let me talk to him."

He went into the door at the corner of the finished end of the office building. Hewitt and Fox dismounted and, after a moment, the old man who had brought the letter did so, too. The foreman was not long inside the office.

"Let me have somebody take care of your horses," he said. "No use putting them up because you're not going to be around here very long, anyway."

He put his fingers in his mouth and whistled an earsplitting blast. He waved his arms and three men stopped work on the other end of the office building and came trotting to him.

"You hold these horses," he said, "and you two pass the word to stop work and stand by. We've got a couple of pil-

grims here that may think they're going to cause trouble."
He jerked a thumb at Hewitt, Fox and the old man. "This
way."

He went into the office ahead of them and did not bother
to hold the door open for them. Hewitt nodded for the
other two to enter first. He went in behind them and closed
the heavy plank door.

He was in the timekeeper's and paymaster's office. Five
men worked here at the payroll and cost books, behind a
peeled-log railing that had been rubbed shiny by the fric-
tion of bodies of men passing through for their pay enve-
lopes.

Behind them was another door to an inner office, and
standing in the open doorway was a man wearing a black
eye patch. If the eyes were the windows of the soul—which
Hewitt did not believe—a one-eyed man had an advantage
on anyone trying to read character at a glance. Hewitt had
learned to study a man's mouth. Either he controlled it or
his emotions did, and either way you learned more than
you could from his eyes.

A. B. Creed, also known as Bob Stanley, also known as
Pearl Butler, and no doubt also known by many another
name in his time, was not a big man. Nor was he a handsome man, but he had a panther look that might stun a
Pretty Bridget. He wore boots and unpressed black pants
and a striped shirt and a hand-stitched weskit, and there
were pearl cuff links in the shirt.

This was neither a roughneck lumberman nor a mere
business executive, but a man who was at home in either
role. He reminded Hewitt of pictures he had seen of Sal-
mon P. Chase, whom Lincoln had appointed Chief Justice
of the United States—the same self-possessed, New Eng-
land sternness of purpose and the same look of concen-

trated power. But Creed had also the mouth of a man Hewitt had once arrested for having murdered three persons to escape serving a one-year jail sentence. It was the grim, controlled mouth of a man who could not think of himself as a loser in a trap.

"What the hell is happening here?" he said in almost a whisper, and he looked at Hewitt when he said it.

"The name," Hewitt said, "is Jefferson Hewitt, Bankers Bonding and Indemnity Company."

"I was told that already. What identification do you have and what is it to me, anyway?"

"I don't need any identification, sir. I have a letter for you from your financial agent in Sacramento. I haven't bothered to open it, but I can tell you what's in it. Your loans are being called because the collateral you put up for them has become worthless. Walkashaw Remedy stock is a drug on the market. You're broke, and in Sacramento and San Francisco they're already fighting over who is going to run this operation," Hewitt said.

"There's also a fellow on the way here for a showdown with you, and I think he's a greater danger to you than all the banks in the world. His real name is Cleve Huks, but he also goes by the name of Durango Slim. My principal mission in California is to arrest him or kill him, and he knows it. He's going to expect you to protect him, and if you don't, he's going to talk.

"Not that there is anything he could tell us that we don't already know. Jack Purefoy is dead. Pretty Bridget's place is closed down and Rozeen has left town, gone where you'll never find her. I suppose you'll want to verify part of this by reading your letter, but I give you my word, it's a waste of time.

"This is as far as you go, you son of a bitch, and if you

make me kill you, you'll be number nine. The point I'm trying to make, Mr. Creed—or Mr. Butler, or Mr. Stanley, or
whatever other name you have—is that you're free to do
whatever you think you can safely do."

He held out the letter. "Your letter, sir. Believe me, it's a
pleasure to deliver this one."

The red-shirted camp boss had shifted toward Hewitt,
but a glance from Creed's one eye stopped him. Creed took
a big clasp knife from his pocket to slit the brown envelope,
but then he did not take the letter out.

"Rozeen, she's gone, you say?" he asked.

"Gone," said Hewitt.

"I don't believe you!"

"Ask Chief Fox. Pretty Bridget's place is but a memory."

"It's the God's truth, Mr. Creed," Fox said. "But I'll tell
you straight, I think your worst worry is this Durango Slim
feller. I've seen some of his work. It wasn't pretty. If he's on
your trail, I'd say he's your first problem."

Hewitt thought that some of the color receded from
Creed's face, but he showed emotion in no other way as he
began reading the letter. He might have been reading a
note inviting him to a tea party, for all the response he be-
trayed. He finished the letter quickly, folded it with steady
hands and replaced it in the envelope.

"I don't understand about Rozeen," he said to Hewitt. "I
find it impossible to believe she'd leave without giving me a
forwarding address. You must have terrified her."

"You bet your life I did! All I had to do was tell her
about Durango Slim. If you can't protect women from your
business associates, you shouldn't steal them."

The strange thing was that with his dream of financial empire in ruins, Creed still could think only of Rozeen. To
Hewitt she had been a very ordinary woman, not particu-

larly attractive, certainly not very bright. Yet she had something—or *had* had it—that enslaved two men as different as Peter O'Hara and this looter of millions with the one eye.

"I suppose," Creed said, "that there is no use asking you where she went."

"None. She wouldn't want to see you. Get it into your head, she's through with you."

"Well, my lord, I'll have to think about this," Creed said, quite calmly. "Excuse me a moment."

He turned and went into his private office, closing the door. Zeno Fox started to follow him, but Hewitt shook his head. The red-shirted camp boss plucked at Hewitt's arm.

"He's got a gun in there, Mr. Hewitt," he said. "If he comes out shooting, now, damn it, I can't let you—"

The gunshot that came from behind the closed door roared like nearby thunder. The camp boss made a leap at the door. Hewitt caught him by the arm.

"Hold it!" he said. "There's nothing you can do in there. It's better this way. You've got a lot of men out there who are going to need some leadership and advice now. They'll listen to you, and—"

"Get your goddamned hands off me!"

The camp boss shoved Hewitt aside and flung the door open. The office stank of gunsmoke. Creed had taken time to close the heavy canvas drapes across the one big window. Chief Fox opened them while Hewitt and the camp boss ran around the desk.

Creed had seated himself at his desk and had held the .45 centered exactly against his heart, with his thumb on the trigger. There had been no death spasm. He had simply slumped down in the big chair, his hand with the gun still in it, his thumb through the trigger guard, falling to his lap.

Even as they watched, his head slumped to one side and a trickle of blood began rolling from his open mouth.

It was a big, hand-made chair of polished redwood, with back and bottom cushions that were already blood-soaked. On the redwood desk stood a cabinet photograph of a woman of middle age, posed with her arms across the shoulders of a boy of about ten and a girl of about eight. To judge by the woman's dress, the picture had been taken at least ten years ago.

"There's nothing you can do for him," Hewitt said sharply, to the camp boss, "and it's pretty clear that you're the man in the spotlight now. What'll the crew do when they find out what that shot was?"

"String you up, probably," the camp boss replied, savagely. "Good lord, man, there go their jobs, don't you realize that? With Mr. Creed dead, what happens to the sawmill?"

Already they could hear heavy boots in the time and pay office. The five clerks behind the railing could not possibly cope with the roughnecks who would come pouring in now. Hewitt took the camp boss by the arm and spun him around. When the man clubbed his fist and tried to jab at his face, Hewitt swung the sap and caught him lightly on the side of his head.

Down the big man went. Fox helped Hewitt haul him to his feet again. "Listen to me, listen to me!" Hewitt said in the man's ear. "Nobody's going to lose a day's work or a day's pay. Why, there are millionaires fighting right now to see who gets to continue this job. What's your name?"

"Dan Casey," the camp boss said, thickly. He was still half-stunned by the rap on the head.

"Listen, Dan, you're the only one who can quiet these fellows down. Get out there and tell them that Creed had gone broke, and that the only man who can save their jobs wants to talk to them. Make that clear to them—their jobs *can* be saved and I'm the *only* man who can do it, and I want to talk to them."

"How do I know?"

"You take my word, that's all. If those men start a lynch party over this damned whelp's suicide, where do you think you'll fit in? You were in here with us. If they burn the place down, who do you think will invest a dime to finish building it? Get out there!"

"You'll talk to them, though? I can't make them believe anything."

"But you can make them listen. Do you want to save your own job, or don't you?"

He literally pushed Casey out the door and closed it behind him. He could hear Casey talking to the men, herding them outside ahead of him.

"What's next?" Zeno Fox asked.

"Watch the door. Don't let anyone in here. You might tell one of the clerks to bring a gunny sack or two, as soon as it quiets down out there."

While Fox guarded the door and sent for the sacks, Hewitt began piling Creed's files on the desk. He had not the time to go through them now, but he saw enough to convince him that here lay the records—the only records—of three massive promotions.

The sawmill proposition might be the richest and Walkashaw Remedy Company the one that would get first attention from the bankers who were sweating blood now. But what most interested Hewitt was a set of sixteen small pocket ledgers, all in a code of some kind. This would be something for Conrad Meuse to pore over, the kind of game he enjoyed and usually won. It would take Conrad about half a day to come up with a complete key to the code.

When that happened, Hewitt was sure, they would have in their hands the record of a methodical merchandiser in women and girls. At least two thousand of them. Their origins. How recruited and at what cost. Their earnings while in the United States. The price they brought when put aboard ship on what would prove to be the last stage of their miserable journeys through life.

Hewitt got outside just in time. Casey's wits had cleared. He was standing on the split-log porch of the office, pleading with the men not to do anything rash and hasty. "The man who can explain it all will be out in a minute," he was saying in his deep, carrying voice when Hewitt came out. "And I promise you—ah, here he is now!"

An ominous roar went up when Hewitt came out and closed the door behind him. It was a sound that might have come from a cage of half-starved, wild animals, and it had Casey frightened. Hewitt knew that to show timidity now was to lose the whole thing.

He smiled widely at them and reached into his pocket for a cigar. He took his time lighting it and then stood with it clenched between his teeth, still smiling, his hands gripping the lapels of his jacket. He was not half as confident as he looked; but you played your hand as though you had aces back to back, and if you lost . . .

So far he never had. "Men," he said, when they would let him, "I'll bet a dollar that most of you have sisters and mothers and sweethearts, and some of you wives. A damned scoundrel who built his fortune on making whores out of honest women has just shot himself like the coward he was. White slavery money started this lumber company, but it will never finish it. That's the promise Dan Casey was trying to make to you when I came out.

"I'm a partner in a bonding company that does business with banks all over the West. Our job is to back honest bankers and weed out the dishonest ones. I've been doing that for twenty years, boys. When I go into a bank, they sweat. When I come out smiling, everybody in that bank is smiling, too.

"I can telegraph for money enough to pay you all for three weeks, out of my own funds, and have that money in Sacramento twenty-four hours after I send my wire. But all that is unnecessary. Right now, five banks in Sacramento and San Francisco are fighting to see which one gets to pour more money into this job and finish this sawmill and get to cutting lumber. We're going to see more—"

From somewhere in that mob of hardcases came a shout, "Let's string him up. He's the one killed Mr. Creed! Mr. Creed told us—didn't he?—that the bankers were trying to steal his company. Kill the son of a bitch!"

"Take that gun away from that man before he gets all of you in trouble," Hewitt said, raising his voice only slightly.

For a split second it could have gone either way. Someone shouted, "Ah, shut up, Ferguson. Let's hear what the man has to say. Get his gun, somebody!"

They muscled the man down by sheer weight. Hewitt kept puffing on his cigar and smiling. When it was silent again, he said:

"I think you boys had better pick a committee of five or six to come in and see Creed for yourselves. Talk to your paymaster and time clerk. They'll tell you that he was in the room by himself—that he committed suicide like the coward he was. I'll tell you this much—it takes a *man* to run something like this, and if any of you wonder if I'm big enough for the job, let's go out there in the soft dirt and settle it right now.

"Because I'm running this until the new bosses take over, with new money from the banks. Don't make any mistake about what I mean, boys—*I'm running it!*"

That's what they wanted to hear, that someone was able to run their tough, brutal world up here in the big timber. Another day, he thought, another dollar. Too bad Conrad couldn't have been here. . . .

CHAPTER XV

Zeno Fox, a tireless man despite his age, started back to Sacramento that evening, accompanied by five Washos who had turned up soon after Hewitt got the gang to go back to work. He carried with him a note from Hewitt to Archie Chancellor, saying: *Chief Fox will tell you what happened here. Urge you to move fast to take over this company. My firm will assist. What we need first is a good lumberman on the site here. Send one.*

Fox also carried a telegram to go to Meuse:

CHANCELLOR OF SACRAMENTO SPECIE BANK ORGANIZING
NEW COMPANY TAKE OVER PRICELESS LUMBERING ASSETS
STOP RECOMMEND RUMFORD FIVE AND FIVE STOP EXPECT
CONCLUDE SI RANKIN JOB SOONEST BUT MUST STAY
HERE UNTIL LUMBER DEAL CLOSED STOP SHIPPING CARTON
EXTREME VALUE WELLS FARGO SECURE AND DECODE
WHEN RECEIVED

"Rumford five and five" referred to a deal in which Bankers Bonding and Indemnity Company had participated nearly ten years ago. Hewitt had dug up information about a big Montana cattle ranch that was going broke. Meuse had organized a corporation to take it over, putting up 5 per cent of the capital and taking another 5 per cent of the stock in return for the information.

Conrad would shriek when he found out how much 5 per

cent of this deal was going to cost, and Chancellor would shriek when he heard that BB&I expected 5 per cent in return for services already rendered and information already given. Fine, let Conrad and Chancellor butt heads by wire.

On a fine pack mule taken from the Creed stables, Fox also carried the box of coded records taken from Creed's desk, to be shipped to Conrad by express.

By daylight one of the Washos had come back with a note from Fox. The chief had met Ed Parry's party and had had a long talk with the marshal. Ed had been overtaken by Sheriff Ernie Goodin, who was giving up the chase because he had come to the approximate border between Sacramento and Amador counties.

The truth was, Fox wrote, that the sheriff had lost heart for the chase when, unexpectedly, he flushed Durango Slim. Singlehandedly, armed only with two .45 revolvers, Durango Slim had stood off the entire posse. He had escaped while the sheriff's men were seeking cover, and was clearly at large in the Sierra Nevada.

What was more to the point, he seemed to know where he was going. He would cross a triangular corner of Amador County into Calaveras County, and then shortly would strike the same oxcart log road that Hewitt and Fox had followed.

The men had gone to work at daylight. When they came in for dinner shortly before noon, Hewitt again made a brief speech to them. He thanked them for the way they had gone at their work—and in this he was completely sincere. They had taken his word that he would see that they were paid, and had pitched in with spirit.

"All that is in the past, boys," he said, pointing to the little mound that marked A. B. Creed's ignoble grave. "This company has a glorious future, and so does every man who helps it through these hard times. But there's one problem we still have, and I need your help with it."

He described Durango Slim and told them of his crimes. "He doesn't know that his old pal Creed is dead," he said. "He's going to come in here looking for a friend, and I don't want any of you taking a chance on getting killed. There's a United States marshal on his tail, with a posse, but he probably doesn't know that and I don't want him to know it.

"I've been on his trail myself for nearly four months, and as soon as I have eaten, I'm going to hit the hay and sleep until somebody wakes me up to tell me that this son of a bitch is coming close to this camp. You'll know it when the Washos tell you. I want somebody to wake me up immediately.

"But don't fool with this fellow! I've been in the man-hunting game for twenty years, and this is the worst, most cold-blooded killer I have ever dealt with. Let's have no heroes, now. Just let me sleep while he wears himself and his horse out, and let me handle him."

The men looked to Dan Casey for guidance. He waved his big ham of a hand at them. "Do as Mr. Hewitt tells you, boys," he said. "Our job is to build a sawmill. Leave Durango Slim to him."

Creed had had his own bedroom back of his office, and Hewitt had appropriated it for his own. He slept in his clothing, on top of the blankets, with his boots by the side of the big, comfortable bed. He had always been able to relax when he had the chance, and wake up when he wanted to. He decided that he needed four hours of sleep desperately.

Sixty seconds after he had stretched out on the bed he was asleep. Four hours later he awakened with the westerly sun on his face from the window. He slipped into his boots and went into the pay office. A glance at the faces of the clerks told him that no word had come from the Washos who were keeping Durango Slim under surveillance.

He drew soap, a towel and clean underwear from the company store. The cooks began frying beefsteak and eggs for him while he went to the creek for a quick bath. The icy water revived him, made him feel better than he had felt in months.

He sent for Dan Casey to eat with him. It was clear that the camp boss still had reservations about him. He did not switch loyalties easily, but that was fine with Hewitt. With Creed dead, there was not much Casey could do but go along with him.

He did his best to make friends with the man as they ate. He did not talk business. He talked about white slavery, about Si Rankin's granddaughter, about Peter O'Hara's wife who had been stolen from him by the kingpin of all white slavers, A. B. Creed.

"I don't know anything about that," Casey said, sullenly. "I build and run sawmills, and I've got some gang saws to install and I should be at it."

"Fine, fine," Hewitt said. "Just try to see that none of your men are murdered by Durango Slim. You see, Dan, you've got to take sides whether you want to or not. I'm not forcing you to—he is. He's coming here expecting protection from his old friend Creed. Better be deciding what you're going to do if he puts the proposition to you."

"I'll know how to answer him, Mr. Hewitt."

"I'm sure you do. Just try to stay alive long enough to do so."

Without Hewitt asking them, the crew worked far into the night, rushing construction of both machinery and the buildings to house it. Hewitt and Casey spent two hours after supper in the office, going over plans. There were changes Casey wanted to make in Creed's designs. It was plain that Creed had been short of money and had been cutting corners.

"Go ahead, do it your way," Hewitt said. "We'll find that the money is there when we need it."

"I want to explain why this will be cheaper in the long run than—"

"Don't bother. You know more about it than I do. Let's do it right while we're doing it."

Casey did not mellow perceptibly, but before leaving the office he slapped his hip to show that he was carrying a .32 revolver. "First time I've gone armed on a job in fifteen years," he said.

Hewitt shook his head. "Don't take too much comfort from that gun, Dan. You're not going to get close enough to Durango Slim to do any good with it. He'll be carrying two forty-fives, and I tell you, man, he's desperate! What has he got to lose if he kills a few more of you?"

Hewitt walked through the dark camp a little before midnight. He was pleased to see that Casey had posted guards here and there, and that they were not recklessly making themselves conspicuous. Casey gave up hard, Hewitt thought with a grin. He would never admit it, but he was convinced.

He walked up to the skid road down which logs now came to be snaked aboard the oxcarts, and stood there a moment, looking down at the sleeping camp. Only a few lights showed—in the kitchen, where cooks were baking bread for tomorrow, and in the office, where one lantern, turned low, burned all night.

He grinned again, thinking how horrified Conrad would

be to know that he had taken command of a gigantic lumbering operation—about which he knew nothing—in the
name of a company that did not yet exist. If he stayed here
all summer, he would have to build a railroad, too. A man
could get into some of the damnedest—

"Hewitt," a soft voice said.

He threw himself to the ground and rolled toward the
deeper shadows under the trees, clawing at his .45. He
thumbed back the hammer, groping with his left hand for
the hat that he had lost.

Lord Cecil McTigue stepped out of the shadows into the
moonlight, his wide-brimmed hat low on his head, a heavy
coat thrown over his shoulders. "You sure scare easy," he
said in his soft voice.

Hewitt got to his feet, holstering the gun. "You just bet I
do," he said.

The Washo's dark eyes had a twinkle in them under the
shadow of his hat brim. "That fella," he said.

"Durango Slim?"

"Yeah. He lose his horse, but he know where he go. Be
here, I think, mebbe by morning."

No use asking how Durango Slim had lost his horse.
Chances were some Washo had gained one. The Indian
walked down to the lumber camp with Hewitt but refused
to come into the bunkhouse while Hewitt roused Dan
Casey.

"I don't know what more I can do, Mr. Hewitt," Casey
said. "I've got six men with rifles out."

"If they were my men," said Hewitt, "I'd make the
rounds and warn them to be extra alert. You can get care-
less, standing sentry go. Let's don't get anyone killed."

Casey dressed, and this time he belted on a .45. He
walked with Hewitt and the Washo about the camp, and

the Indian's special wariness made Casey seek the shadows, too. Sure enough, they found one man sitting on a stump in the dark with his back against a shed wall, sound asleep.

Casey jerked him to his feet and shook him violently, cursing under his breath. "I ought to let the son of a bitch ambush you," he said. "Close your eyes one second more, and if Durango Slim doesn't kill you, I will."

Now there was nothing to do but wait. Hewitt tried to question the Washo, but either he did not have the English to understand and respond or he simply did not want to. The three of them went to the cookhouse and had coffee and fresh cinnamon rolls together. Lord Cecil was in no hurry to go. Whatever was going to happen would happen here, he seemed sure.

Hewitt returned to his room behind the office, pulled off his boots and went to sleep again. Between Casey and the Indian, nothing would be overlooked, and he had never been a worrier when he had good men on the job.

It was gunfire that awakened him: the heavy, harsh bark of a .45—then another—and then the heavier slam of a rifle. A man began screaming, trying to call a name that he never did get out because after three long, tearing screams he died.

Hewitt rolled out of bed and stepped into his boots and hit the floor running. One whole end of the camp seemed to go up in a burst of flame the color and shape of a peony. The shock wave of an explosion raced toward him as he opened the office door, and threw him back against the wall.

There was dynamite stored here somewhere—he knew that much. Or there had been. Every lumber camp needed dynamite now and then. When his ears stopped ringing he heard two more gunshots and then . . . silence.

CHAPTER XVI

It took interminable minutes to get the story straight. Early daylight had come, revealing the crater gouged out by the explosion. Several trees had fallen into it and caught fire and the fire threatened to spread to the cordwood pile that was being accumulated to feed the steam engines, but Casey already had a bucket brigade working between the creek and the fire.

"He knows something about dynamite, you can be sure of that," he shouted into Hewitt's ear, over the roar of the flames. "He found the powder house in the dark. Near as I can make out, one of my men challenged him."

"Instead of shooting on sight," Hewitt said.

"Correct," Casey said, grimly. "Now the son of a bitch is gone, got away clean. He just beat the living hell out of one of my men. Let's see what he can tell us."

One sentry dead, shot through the belly, but Durango Slim had not got away with his rifle, at least. This was the man Hewitt had heard screaming. After death, his body had been thrown more than a hundred yards by the force of the explosion.

About the time the dynamite went off, Durango Slim apparently had been heading for the horse corrals. Another sentry spotted him and snapped a couple of shots at him. Durango Slim dived into the timber. A third sentry came running, armed only with a .45.

The two conferred briefly, their ears still ringing and their minds still half-stunned by the blast. The one with the rifle thought he saw a figure at the corrals. He raced toward it, leaning forward and keeping his head down in the watery, early daylight. Just in time, he saw that it was one of the hostlers in the corral, ready to open the gate and free the horses if that became necessary.

The other man waited one second too long. He had the .45 in his hand when Durango Slim jumped him from behind and clubbed him down with something. When the man came to, Durango Slim was sitting on his chest with his knife in his hand.

"Where's Creed?" he demanded when he saw that the sentry was conscious.

"Dead."

Durango Slim raised the knife. The sentry thought he was a dead man, but Durango Slim only brought his fist down to crush the sentry's nose.

"God damn you, where's Creed?" he snarled.

The sentry could have strangled on blood from his own nose. Durango Slim had to turn him over on his stomach to let him breathe. He used the blunt end of the knife handle to pound the man around the back of the head.

"Honest to God," the sentry said, "he's dead. I can show you where he's buried. Right there, yander."

"Then who's in charge here? Who runs it when Creed's gone?"

"Man by the name of Hewitt is running it now."

"*Hewitt?*"

Durango Slim went crazy. He beat the man senseless and left him there. Lord Cecil McTigue followed his tracks down toward the horse corrals. There Durango Slim had waited behind a tree, sizing up his chances. Now two hostlers were in plain sight, pacing the corrals warily.

Hewitt had never claimed to be a wilderness tracker, but when the Washo pointed out Durango Slim's dilemma, Hewitt could see it, too. Either of the hostlers would have been a difficult shot with only a side arm—both, an impossible one. There was no way to slip up on them with a knife. Even if he had been able to dispose of them, he still would have had to choose a horse, saddle and bridle him, and get away on him.

"He run like hell," Lord Cecil McTigue said.

"Where to? Where can he go from here?" Hewitt asked.

The Indian did not answer immediately. He plunged into the brush under the virgin forest and in a moment or two found Durango Slim's tracks. Even Hewitt could see that the fugitive was indeed running like hell, putting as much distance between him and the seething camp as he could. He came to the skid road above the camp, crossed it and kept running.

In the rapidly brightening daylight that was blotting out the fog that hung under the trees, the trail was plain enough. Durango Slim, no woodsman, would be disoriented at least until the sun rose above the Sierra peaks. But Hewitt thought he would keep climbing, putting himself above pursuit as he tried to search out a cleft that would lead him to the eastern slope of the range.

Casey was anxious to get back to the camp and straighten up the chaos there. "Go on, you're in charge," Hewitt told him. "This fellow is my job. Maybe Lord Cecil will help me. We'll get a couple of horses and go after him."

"No horse," said the Washo. "Better we walk."

"Why?"

"He think we take horse. He look for man on horse to chase him. Better we fool him, eh?"

"He's right, Dan," said Hewitt. "We'll go back and eat something and pack some grub. Let him run his guts out while we're having a good breakfast."

"You sure you're up to it?" Casey asked, with a frown. "These Indians can walk your tail off."

"But Durango Slim can't. This is just the way I like it."

They returned to the camp. The entire crew had turned out and, to a man, were more interested in tracking down Durango Slim than in restoring order there. Casey clubbed a hickory pick handle and offered to brain any man who started out of the camp. He bellowed his orders at them. To hell with the crater that had been the powder house. The fire was already under control—wet it down good and get back to work. Anybody who felt like arguing, get himself a pick handle and try his luck.

There was roast beef hash to be warmed up, and a pot of brown beans to fry. While the cook prepared their breakfast and a bait of trail grub, Hewitt filled his pockets with .45 ammunition and gave the Washo another .45 from company stores.

"No rifle?" the Washo asked, softly.

"No. I want to be close enough to him to know he can hear me," Hewitt replied.

The Indian almost smiled. They took their time eating. The cook tied a pot of beans and a pot of hash up in a gunny sack with a single shoulder rope that held the lids on tightly. Hewitt finished eating, stood up and threw the rope over his shoulder.

"You ain't gonna tell Dan you're leavin'?" the cook asked.

"He knows," said Hewitt. "You don't have to draw Casey any pictures."

They slipped out of the kitchen and headed for the corrals, Lord Cecil McTigue taking the lead. The Washo did not bother to glance down at the ground until they had again crossed the skid road, and it seemed to Hewitt that he barely glanced at it as he headed up the slope beyond.

The first direct rays of sunlight suddenly broke through when they were high above the camp. Blue jays were long since awake and screaming insults at them from the trees. Gray squirrels chattered at them. Not a breath of wind moved through the huge pines. Far below them, the big, sprawling camp looked like a child's toy village. Casey already had the boiler fired up to power the winch that would drag the sills of the saw bed into position. The thin thread of gray smoke had to rise high before there was enough air movement to form it into a lazy, hooked cloud like a question mark.

The Indian touched Hewitt's arm. Hewitt turned his back on the camp and they began climbing again. Lord Cecil McTigue again paid little attention to the ground in front of him. When he wanted to find the sign Durango Slim had left behind, he found it. But mostly he remained on guard against ambush, his sharp, slate-colored eyes endlessly ransacking the cover from which a shot might come.

Quickly Hewitt got the knack of it. You did not have to bother to put yourself in the fugitive's place and ask yourself what you would do. If you were like Lord Cecil McTigue, you knew. And just kept going.

Late afternoon found them descending a steep canyon wall where the timber was so heavy that they could literally only see from tree to tree. They had stopped to rest only briefly, leaning against trees to spoon out handfuls of the beans and hash. Hewitt was satisfied with the job of work his own body was turning in today. The long pursuit of Virginia Baldwin's murderer had melted every gram of fat on him, had left him gaunt and yet tough enough to bring a look of respect to this tough old Washo's eyes.

A huge sow grizzly with three cubs crashed through the underbrush ahead of them. The impatience with which she scolded her young'ns into flight was almost human. Suddenly she reared up on her hind legs, bigger than life and beautiful in a strange savage way, no more than a hundred feet away.

Lord Cecil McTigue froze on his feet. So did Hewitt. The bear's eyesight was bad, Hewitt knew, but there was nothing wrong with her nose. She knew they were there.

But somehow she sensed that they were no threat to her and her cubs. She dropped down to all four feet and ran after the cubs, not bothering to thread a path through the brush. She simply smashed her way through it. Hewitt waited, his eyes on the motionless Washo.

When the Indian turned around and looked at Hewitt, he was smiling. "Some big," he whispered, but there was not fear so much as admiration in his face. As though he and the bear were friends whose chance meeting in the forest had left them still friends.

"I hope Durango Slim has sense enough to stay out of her way," Hewitt said.

Lord Cecil McTigue walked on. "You never can tell," he said, over his shoulder.

They saw no more of the grizzly, but shortly before night fell they found Durango Slim's tracks just where the Indian expected to find them. He got down on hands and knees to study them, crawling along and chuckling softly in his throat. He stood up and dusted off his hands.

"How far ahead of us is he, do you think?" Hewitt asked.

"Too close," the Washo replied.

Hewitt looked up to where the inky treetop shadows had closed over him. "So we camp here," he said.

"Sure. Don't want him in the dark, eh?"

The Indian sat down and made himself comfortable. That simply he made camp. There would be no fire tonight, probably not even conversation between them. When you came to a stopping place on a hot trail, you just stopped.

Hewitt sat down, too. "What's ahead of us?"

Lord Cecil McTigue pointed. "Nice little river there."

"How far?"

"Oh—thirty minute."

"Hard to cross?"

Lord Cecil McTigue shook his head. "No. He on the other side now. We cross before morning sun. Son of a bitch got to rest sometime, eh? Be plenty ready when he cross river."

"I see."

"Him sleep there, us sleep here, you see?"

"I see. What's on the other side?"

"Big climb."

"How long will that take us?"

"Oh—couple hours. Go slow. Don't want to find the son of a bitch when he's ahead of us and higher up."

"Then what?"

Lord Cecil McTigue had been carrying the grub. He took time to open it now, making sure he did not betray where they were by clinking pot against lid. The pots were still more than half full. He offered them to Hewitt, who shook his head and waved his hand: You first.

"Something I want you see," the Indian said.

"What?"

"You see, all right. Where we catch him, I mean."

"What is it?"

But the Indian had said all he meant to say. In his mind, Hewitt thought, Lord Cecil McTigue had it all planned, but for reasons of his own he did not want to talk about it now. And when a man could do the things that this one could do, when he so clearly had made a judgment based on values of his own, you had to respect him. All right, we do it his way. . . .

Hewitt ate sparingly of the beans and hash. He would have appreciated a drink of water and a chance to wash his hands afterward, but he had to respect the Washo in that matter, too. The nearest water was probably the river that now separated them from a starved, exhausted, terrified and desperate man. Let him rest there, then. Let him throw himself down, soaked to the skin, too tired to go another step and fearful not to.

Let him sleep, if he could. Let him dream if he did sleep. Let him remember Peter O'Hara, and how it had felt to drive the knife into him.

Let him remember Simon C. Rankin's daughter, the spoiled and willful and now dead Emma. Let him remember Emma's daughter, who had stood up to him at last and who had died resisting him.

Let him lie there with his cheek pressed against the deep forest duff, his fingers digging into it for a handhold and grip that he would never find. Let him shiver with cold and fear, let him sweat faster than the night air could dry his clothing, let him try, only try, to get his nerve up for the showdown tomorrow.

The end of the trail was just that close. Hewitt could sleep while the Indian kept watch. Sleep and rest, as Durango Slim never could.

CHAPTER XVII

It would be a river only at this time of year, with the snow melting higher each day on the mountains and the runoff picking up force and volume. It was wider and deeper than Lord Cecil McTigue had expected, but it had to be crossed in the dark. They would be helpless if they were caught out in the middle of it with Durango Slim on the other bank.

The Washo groped his way up and down the bank uncertainly and then, saying nothing, took his gun out and held it over his head as he waded in. Hewitt walked in behind him. The current caught him and threatened to throw him off his feet, but he leaned against it and was even able to give the Indian some help when they reached the middle. He had to grab fast when he grabbed, catching the Indian by the hair with his left hand and steadying them both for one perilous moment.

Then the Indian got his balance again and plunged on. The water came almost to their armpits at its deepest, but Hewitt estimated that it was no more than seventy or eighty feet across. And cold! And it seemed colder still when they came out on the other side and clambered up the bank where the morning breeze could catch them.

No time to get warm, however. The Indian plunged into the brush as though he knew where he was going. Daylight found them panting up a steep ridge, feeling their way a step at a time. Suddenly Lord Cecil McTigue stopped.

"Wait here, eh?" he said. "Better eat, too, I guess. Then we find this son of a bitch's tracks."

Hewitt's clothing was almost dry, but he was still cold and the last of the cold hash and beans did not warm him. He covered the pans with leaves, just in case Durango Slim was behind them and should come across them, and picked out landmarks whereby he could find them again.

Shortly he could see the river they had crossed in the dark. It tumbled across a narrow, rocky mountain meadow too short to be called a canyon, and spilled over the edge of an unseen brink of some kind under the trees. The roar of the water somehow seemed louder up here than it had down there last night.

They waited. Now and then Lord Cecil McTigue stood up carefully to look around him. The sun burst through the gaps in the range above them and burned out the morning fog.

"You hear that?" the Indian murmured.

Over the racket of the water, Hewitt could hear the squawking of blue jays. He grinned at the Indian. "They found him for us," he said.

"Yes, yander."

The Washo pointed. By his reckoning, Durango Slim was less than a quarter of a mile from them at about the same elevation, in a magnificent stand of young sugar pine. A tall white stob of a dead tree towered over everything. More than fifty years ago, a big burn had raced through here, killing everything. All those young giants had sprouted since then. The ghostly white stob was the last one still standing of the forest that had been killed by the fire.

Even as they watched, the stob's dead roots gave way suddenly. Who knew why a tree that had lived for a hundred years, and then stood dead for half that long, would fall at a given second? It toppled in silence, crashed through the young, living trees in silence and vanished forever from their sight.

Then the noise of its falling rolled toward them like thunder.

They began walking, edging toward the dead tree as they climbed. They intercepted Durango Slim's trail considerably above where the tree had fallen, and shortly after that were at the top of the ridge.

They plunged down the other side. Lord Cecil McTigue stepped aside to let Hewitt take the lead. Durango Slim's trail was plain here. Slim was walking the stiff walk of an exhausted man, digging his heels in hard and trying to thread his way through the easiest parts of the brush.

The Indian touched Hewitt's shoulder. "Look," he whispered.

Hewitt raised his eyes from the trail and knew why the Washo had not tried to tell him last night what was on the other side of the ridge. Through the tall stems of the pines loomed something too big and beautiful to grasp quickly, let alone understand.

There it stood, the biggest and oldest living thing in the world—the mountain redwood, *Sequoia gigantea*. Dozens of them marched on and on through a sea of blooming dogwood and azaleas, in a glade where debris from dying trees had enriched the soil for three thousand years. The russet trunks, some of them thirty feet in diameter, glowed like newly shined leather in the morning sunlight.

O'Hara's South Grove? Hewitt would have bet on it.

His eyes went up and up to where the first limb grew, a shaft of wood thicker than any of the pines that shared the glade. The crowns of the trees merged with the very sky, giving it a solid anchor to the granite spine of the Sierra

Nevada. The nearest tree was obviously hollow, for a good way up from the ground. Its interior had burned out long ago, a wound that would have wiped out any lesser thing.

But, he had heard, fire only got rid of the dead punk-wood that was inhabited by destructive insects, leaving an encircling wall of living timber four to a dozen feet thick around a vault like—like O'Hara's cathedrals? And instead of dying like the pines, which had to be renewed by seedlings, the sequoias died again and again and yet went on living as fire purged their dead parts. Even as he watched, he knew, they were growing—second by second, reaching for still greater heights, still another century.

"Not many your people see this," the Indian whispered. "Maybe five, maybe ten, maybe fifty—who knows? Hard to come here. Long, long time before your people make trail here, eh?"

Hewitt nodded and pointed to Durango Slim's tracks in the deep duff. Here the fugitive had stood for a moment, unable to believe his own eyes, staring at those massive monsters and wondering if he had gone mad. And then he had plunged on ahead into the teeming, blooming brush. And there he still was.

"Here's where we smoke him out," Hewitt said.

"Yes," Lord Cecil McTigue said. "I wait here."

Meaning, this is your job and I won't interfere because I wouldn't want you to interfere with me.

Hewitt took out his .45 and checked it.

"Durango Slim," he called loudly.

Not a sound, not even a blue jay in this dense thicket.

"End of the trail, Durango Slim," Hewitt shouted. "I'm coming in after you. Fair warning—I'm going to shoot on sight. That's a hell of a lot more warning than you ever gave anyone, isn't it?"

He handed his hat to the Indian to hold. Gun in hand, he inched into the brush, keeping the taller dogwood above his head and trying not to move a leaf to betray him to so much as a blue jay. The thick growth swallowed him so swiftly that after five steps he could not see the Washo when he looked back. On he went, planning each single step carefully, crouching and sidling between saplings and twisting his body to fit the narrow spaces nature had left here.

Again he stopped, and this time he cupped his hands around his mouth, smelling the good gun-oil smell of the .45 in his right hand.

"How about it, Durango Slim—want to make a deal? Like to come out and surrender, with your hands above your head? Take you back to Sacramento and maybe you can beat it in the courts. The Irishman had a gun in his hand. Want to plead self-defense?"

No answer. Hewitt waited a moment.

"Don't want to deal on O'Hara? Then how about the deputy United States marshal? That's two we know about —right? Ready to put your hands up and come in?"

"Hewitt?" came a voice from somewhere deeper in the redwood glade. "Is that you, Hewitt?"

"Bet your life it is!"

"If I come out with my hands up, can we talk about this? I didn't mean to kill that son of a bitch in Sacramento. And I didn't kill any deppity marshal, either! I got a right to a fair trial. If I come out, you won't just gun me down?"

"No, I won't just gun you down. But after you've stood trial for those two, how about going back to Colorado with me to stand trial for the murder of Virginia Baldwin? Still feel like surrendering?"

"I don't make out what you're saying," Durango Slim replied—pleadingly, and too late.

"Oh yes you do," Hewitt called out, "and so we both know that you're not going to come out with your hands up, don't we? I told you, Cleve—it's the end of the trail."

"What did you call me?"

It was a thin, quavering wail and Hewitt did not bother to answer it. It was pretty clear now why Durango Slim had taken the trouble to kill Peter O'Hara—because O'Hara could identify him by his right name and perhaps link him to other crimes.

An inch at a time was the way you did it. This man's death would not help Virginia Baldwin or her mother. But here was a good place to think about them and believe, at last, that they were at peace. Here was a good place to remember Si Rankin, a good thing to tell him about when the time came. Maybe even Si could find peace, when he knew about this great, secret grove.

But still more important were the girls and women still alive and happy, who had a chance to stay that way with these two men dead—the one who called himself Creed a few days ago, and the one who liked to be known as that sport of sports, Durango Slim. You never wiped out prostitution. But you could wipe out a few white slavers who made money by it.

Inch by inch, in perfect silence, squatting and twisting and squirming through the brush, Hewitt again came to where he could see the first redwood. Nothing grew to any height very close to those trees. Between Hewitt and the black-rimmed, fire-formed doorway to the roomy, vaulted interior of that massive hollow trunk there was no cover for a man.

Hewitt waited a long time. He had feeling, somehow, of

being in touch with the Indian—that Lord Cecil McTigue knew exactly what he was doing and would have done it this way himself. There were times when you merely waited.

That time came to an end, and Hewitt stood up with the .45 in his hand. Somehow he knew when it was time to do that, just as the Indian would have.

"You coming out," he called, "or am I going to have to come in there after you?"

A moment of silence.

Durango Slim's nerve cracked and he came out of the wide doorway in the hollow tree with both guns blazing. Hewitt lifted the .45 and thumbed back the hammer, taking his time.

He squeezed off one shot and saw it smack Durango Slim in the chest. He seemed to kick up both legs as though trying to jump free of something as the big slug slammed through him and dropped him on his back.

One leg lifted in a death spasm and dropped. Hewitt holstered the gun. He stood watching a moment, hearing the Indian plowing through the brush behind him. The prying blue jays, guardians of the forest, began screaming their dissent as they coursed toward the big sequoia. They saw the dead man on the ground between his two guns and darted down to investigate a cloud of glittering blue.

When the Washo reached him, the two walked together to the redwood. The Indian led the way into the roomy interior. A dozen people could have lived here comfortably.

"My grandpa's grandpa, him and his wife, they live here once," Lord Cecil McTigue said. "Had to hide out, see? Since long, long time, this where my family keep a hiding place if we need it."

"And you don't want me to tell anyone about it."

"Better if you don't. Long time before anybody find it, and it's a good place to have until then."

Hewitt took a long, careful look about him, trying to fix the glory of this place firmly in his mind, to tell Si Rankin about it. Not how to find it, only to give him, if possible, a little of the serenity and peace of it. A little of the understanding that all things came to an end—even the sequoias.

"I'll keep your secret," Hewitt promised.

They buried Durango Slim as Hewitt and O'Hara had buried Deputy Marshal Joe Crandal, only they had to grub out the grave with their bare hands and carry stones a long way to cover it afterward. The dead man had more than $4,500 in cash on him, some of which he had stolen from Hewitt. Hewitt handed all but $500 of the money to Lord Cecil McTigue.

Sewn into the lining of the dead man's jacket was a small muslin packet containing a few pieces of jewelry. Only one piece amounted to anything, a pearl clip Hewitt was sure had belonged to Emma Rankin Baldwin. He pocketed the clip, to take back to Si, and gave the rest of the things to the Indian.

Inside the hollow tree, he knelt and wrote something with his fingertip in the dirt formed by the decay of ancient debris from the tree's heartwood. As he wrote, he thought of Sam Berry, back in Kelly's Ravine. Sam would understand this. He hoped that Si Rankin would, too.

"That don't last, not long, you know?" Lord Cecil McTigue said.

"I know," Hewitt said, standing up to dust off his hands on his pants legs, "but it's something I have to do for an old man who has lost a daughter and a granddaughter. I wish he could see this place. I think that may make him feel a little better, since he can't."

"Man got to do some things, yes he does," the Indian agreed. "I tell you, none of my people walk on them words, and nobody else know about this. Maybe they last longer than you think."

They walked out of the grove together, leaving behind them, in soft dirt protected by the massive bulk of the big tree, the memorial: *Be at peace, Emma and Virginia.*